The Olden Days Locket

PENNY CHAMBERLAIN

sononis PRESS   WINLAW, BRITISH COLUMBIA

NATIONAL LIBRARY OF CANADA CATALOGUING IN PUBLICATION DATA

Chamberlain, Penny, 1958-
    The olden days locket / Penny Chamberlain.

    ISBN 1-55039-128-3

    1. Point Ellice House (Victoria, B.C.)—Juvenile fiction. I. Title.
PS8555.PZ7.C355301 2002

Sono Nis Press most gratefully acknowledges the support for our publishing
program provided by the Government of Canada through the Book
Publishing Industry Development Program (BPIDP), The Canada Council
for the Arts, and the British Columbia Arts Council.

Edited by Ann Featherstone
Cover and book design by Jim Brennan

First Printing October 2002
Second Printing March 2004

Published by
SONO NIS PRESS
PO Box 160
Winlaw, BC V0G 2J0
1-800-370-5228
books@sononis.com
www.sononis.com

Printed and bound in Canada

The Canada Council | Le Conseil des Arts
for the Arts | du Canada

TABLE OF CONTENTS

for
Katie and Adrian

1

The Girl at the Window

"Hey, Jess! Get out of the way!"

Before Jess could turn around, *WHAM!* A basketball smashed into the the back of her head. It sent a flash through her skull as bright as a shooting star. Down she went sprawling, onto the gym floor.

The hard, polished floor pressed against the side of her face, and the fluorescent lights glared harshly overhead. The red and blue gym lines looked like they were writhing across the floor like slithering snakes. She closed her eyes and felt herself sinking down, down through the floor and into a silent, black fog.

"Jess! Jess? Can you hear me?" The voice came from a long way away. Jess tried to ignore it, but the voice was insistent. "Jess. Open your eyes. Open your eyes."

Her head felt like it was stuffed with wool. She dragged her heavy eyelids partway open. Mrs. Marshall was leaning over her. The whistle hanging from her neck was swinging back and forth, glinting in the light.

"Are you all right?"

"Uh huh, I'm okay," Jess said, but the back of her head was throbbing.

A crowd of curious faces pressed up behind Mrs. Marshall. Maxine and Tiffany were there too, of course, smirking in the background. Jess turned her eyes away, wishing she hadn't made such a fool of herself.

Clumsy! That's how she felt. Clumsy and uncoordinated. She couldn't imagine Maxine or Tiffany getting whacked in the head with a basketball and falling down in front of everyone. Oh no, that would never happen to them. Maxine and Tiffany always looked perfect, like two matching Barbie dolls. Their clothes were always the latest fashion. And they had the same hairstyle—streaked blonde and shoulder-length. Not a strand out of place.

"I think we should take you to the medical room," Mrs. Marshall was saying.

"No, really. I'm fine," said Jess, a little unsteadily. "I just slipped. That's all."

"Sure?"

"Sure."

Mrs. Marshall gave her a reassuring pat on the shoulder then straightened up to blow her whistle. *TWEEEEEET!!!!!* "Okay, everyone. Time's up. Put the balls away and hurry up getting changed. The bus is here to take us to Point Ellice House."

The class was noisy and excited about the field trip. They scrambled to find seats on the bus. Jess picked one by the window, about halfway back.

"Klutz," Maxine said with a sneer as she passed down the aisle.

"Bookworm!" said Tiffany, right behind her.

Jess stared straight ahead as if she hadn't heard them. Then she stole a quick peek over her shoulder. They were at the very back of the bus, looking smug and confident and thoroughly pleased with themselves.

When everyone had sat down, there was one seat left over, the one beside Jess.

Jess turned to look out the window, hoping no one would notice her flushed cheeks. I don't care. It doesn't bother me. She made herself say it a few times in her head, trying to convince herself it was true. Everyone on the whole bus would see the empty seat beside her. Why couldn't someone sit beside her for a change? Would that be so hard? She knew they all thought she was weird. As if there was something wrong with liking books and history, instead of clothes and sports. She could hear them all around her, chattering noisily, happy that they didn't have to be in school.

The bus jerked forward, lurched out of the school parking lot and rumbled onto the street. Soon they were crossing the Point Ellice Bridge. Down below, the waters of the Gorge rippled in millions of shining puckers like scales on a fish. At the end of the bridge, right at the corner, was the sign for Point Ellice House.

The bus turned onto Pleasant Street. Jess sat forward and craned her neck to see better. But Pleasant Street didn't seem very pleasant at all. There was a jangle of ugly, grim metal warehouses, a dusty recycling plant and, at the far end, a huge towering pile of rusted car parts that loomed like some kind of nightmarish mountain.

But it was the right street, only two short blocks. And right in the middle was Point Ellice House, the only house on the entire street. The bus rumbled past a graceful, white picket fence and pulled into the parking lot. Jess could see glimpses of a lush, hidden garden through the trees, the wooden shakes of the rooftop and a red brick chimney.

The class piled out of the bus and Mrs. Marshall herded them up to the front door. Jess stood apart at the back of the line. Somehow, despite the constant chattering of the others, the garden still managed to seem hushed and peaceful. Tall trees screened out the rest of Pleasant Street. There were carefully manicured lawns, flower beds edged with thick, ivy borders and a sweeping, gravelled driveway.

She turned back to face the house. It stretched low to the ground, bulging with bay windows and verandas and painted a soft rosy apricot. The details were picked out in coffee-coloured trim. It was a house that sat comfortably in the garden, the way a contented cat curls into a warm and sunny spot.

The front door swung open and a friendly, middle-aged woman stepped out to greet them. She was wearing a blue-and-white striped apron over a long black skirt. She looked, to Jess, exactly the way a parlourmaid might have looked a hundred years ago.

"Good afternoon. I'm Miss Libby. Welcome to Point Ellice House," she said. "Wipe your feet at the door and come in."

They all crowded into the front hall. It was dark in the house compared to the bright sunshine outside. Jess' eyes adjusted slowly as Miss Libby began telling them about the house.

"The O'Reilly family lived here for over a hundred years. The family kept almost everything—clothes, recipes, diaries, visiting cards. They didn't throw anything away. That's lucky for us because now we have a complete record of life from that period, almost like a time capsule. People can visit the house and see what it was like to live at the turn of the century."

Mrs. Marshall cleared her throat. "Miss Libby, can you explain why a well-to-do family like the O'Reillys would choose to live here, on this street, surrounded by all this industry? We couldn't help but notice it as we drove up today."

"That's a good question," Miss Libby replied. "When the O'Reillys lived here, this neighbourhood was very different. There were beautiful homes on both sides of the Gorge. And there were dinner dances and boating parties and tennis tournaments and afternoon teas. It was a genteel neighbourhood and a lovely way of life.

"But gradually, over the years, more and more industry built up. One by one, the homes were demolished and replaced with sawmills and warehouses and even a tannery. This is the only home left on this side of the water now. Over on the other side of the Gorge, you might have noticed, there are a few Victorian homes left as well."

The other side of the Gorge! Jess lived in an old house on the other side of the Gorge. Maybe her home was one of the places Miss Libby was talking about.

"Now, let's start the tour," Miss Libby said. She directed them to a bedroom door that led off the hallway. "This was the mother's—Caroline O'Reilly's—bedroom." Miss Libby pointed out the warming cupboard for the linens beside the fireplace, and the table at the window where she had written her letters.

Everyone pressed up to have a look. From the back of the crowd Jess could just make out a glimpse of wallpaper—blue-green with tiny gold flowers—but nothing more. She waited until they moved down the hall to the next room.

Then it was Jess' turn to see Caroline's bedroom. The window blinds had been drawn to filter the bright afternoon light. It was an elegant room filled with fine furniture and a richly patterned carpet covering the floor. There was an embroidered silk shawl and fan laid out on the bedspread. It looked as if Caroline O'Reilly might come back into the room at any moment, pick up the fan and the shawl and ready herself for an afternoon outing.

Jess could hear snippets of Miss Libby's comments from down the hall. "The father was Peter O'Reilly. This is his bedroom. You can see it is quite small compared to Mrs. O'Reilly's. There's the footbath by the chair. He used to soak his feet there."

"Eeeeww," someone said. The rest of the class giggled.

"Now, we'll go down the hall a little farther and I'll show you the study and the drawing-room."

The group moved down the hall. Jess lagged behind. She liked looking through each doorway on her own, without anyone else around. She wanted to imagine what it would have been like living in these beautiful rooms—taking a book from the shelf and settling herself in a comfortable chair by the window, or perhaps playing one or two songs on the piano.

But wait! Of course she wouldn't be playing the piano. She could hardly play a note. How did that notion get into her head? Just as she was turning to leave the drawing-room, something caught her eye. It was a painting on the wall, a view of Point Ellice House in the summer. Striped awnings were pulled down to shade the windows. There was a stretch of green lawn and masses of flowers. In fact, as she looked at the vines winding up and around the veranda, it was almost as if she could smell them. Something about the painting stirred up a sense of unease inside her. She felt her stomach rise and fall the way it did on a Ferris wheel. Why would something like an old painting have such an effect?

The class was moving on. Reluctantly Jess pulled

her eyes away from the painting and went to the next room. It was Kathleen's—the daughter's—bedroom. The room was full of lovely things. The washstand set was decorated with painted ribbons, and there were dainty ornaments on the mantle. A strange feeling stirred in the back of Jess' mind. It felt as if, sometime in the past, she had seen this room before. But when? She had only moved to Victoria a year ago. This was her first visit to Point Ellice House.

But the peculiar feeling stuck. It wouldn't go away. The curtains, the white candlewick bedspread, the blue quilted slippers. It felt as if she remembered all these things. Then her eyes fell upon a tiny, grey-and-white china pig standing on the shelf in the far corner of the room. She felt a pang of recognition.

She was certain she had seen that pig before. There was no doubt. She had. She knew she had.

Jess forced herself to take a few slow, deep breaths. Then she walked down the hall to join the rest of the group. They were moving into the servants' area of the house, through the pantry with its wooden sink, the servery, and the kitchen with its big, black stove.

"The O'Reillys had a Chinese cook and houseboy who worked in these rooms," Miss Libby explained. "They also had a parlourmaid and sometimes a gardener."

Although Jess tried to focus on the tour, the strange feeling still troubled her. She wanted to take her time and linger behind in the house. Maybe she had read about Point Ellice House in one of her history books. Or maybe her parents had brought her here when they were on a holiday years ago.

Miss Libby was ushering the class out the scullery's screen door to the back veranda and through the gardens. Jess trailed behind, past the sweet-smelling roses and the clusters of orange poppies with their giant petals that made her think of crepe paper. She followed the group across the croquet lawn to the rose garden near the banks of the Gorge.

"This was one of Kathleen's favourite places," Miss Libby was saying. "She selected many of the rose varieties for this garden."

Jess was only half paying attention. She looked back at the house. From where she stood the view was exactly the same as the painting in the drawing-room. Nothing had changed. Even the flowering vines were still there, climbing up the veranda.

Then Jess noticed something else higher up, just under the roofline. A girl stood at the attic window.

Jess squinted. The girl looked to be about Jess' age. Her face was pale and her hair was fair, flowing down in waves past her shoulders. She was looking through the treetops toward the Gorge. No one else in the class seemed to notice her. Not one head turned in her direction, and Miss Libby continued talking about the garden without a pause. Then the girl stepped back from the window. Even though the afternoon sun was still beating down, the air turned cold for a moment. Jess felt a shiver pass through her.

2

———◆◆◆———

Ghost Story

Jess fidgeted impatiently as she waited for her mom to come home from work. As soon as the door opened, Jess asked, "Mom, have we ever been to Point Ellice House before?"

"Never." Her mother dumped a pile of work files on the hall table and balanced her purse on the top. "How was the field trip today?"

"It was really good. But I keep thinking I've been

there before. It seems like I can remember it."

"Well, we've never been before. Believe me."

Her mom slipped off her shoes, went into the kitchen and started rummaging through the fridge. Her voice came from somewhere deep inside the fridge. "I spent my lunch hour down at the archives doing a bit of research on our house." She pulled out some carrots and then plunged her head back into the fridge. "I found out that a family named Abbott lived here back at the turn of the century." She emerged again with a bag of lettuce. "He was a banker. They had a couple of children."

Jess stood in the kitchen doorway, thinking back over the day's events. She had felt strange ever since she'd been hit by the basketball. Maybe she had a concussion. That could explain everything, couldn't it? Or maybe....

"Mom? What's it called when you think you've been somewhere before, but you haven't? It just seems like you have."

"Déjà vu. It's a trick the mind plays on you. Is that what you mean?"

"I guess so," replied Jess. "I guess that's it."

Jess climbed the stairs to her room. Maybe that's all it was. Déjà vu.

Jess woke up the next morning feeling deliciously happy. It was Saturday morning. No school for two whole days. And after that, only one week left until summer holidays. She stretched luxuriously, sensing the clear, sunny day through her still-closed eyelids.

But when she drew in a deep breath...the peppery smell of sawdust filled her nose. Oh right, the renovation. Her eyes flicked open and her heart sank.

A huge plastic sheet was tacked up across the opening where the wall used to be. Her mom and dad had been working on the renovation for the past month. So far they had knocked down the wall to make her small bedroom and the room next door into one sizable room. There was a sickly, pickle-green wallpaper on her side of the plastic and ugly maroon wallpaper on the other. At the moment the maroon side was cluttered with stepladders and piles of wood and tools. That side was going to be finished first. Then all her things would be moved across when they started work on the green side.

"It'll be great when it's finished," her dad had assured her. "You'll have a much bigger and brighter room, and you can pick out any wallpaper you want."

But in the meantime, all her cherished books had been boxed up and stored in the basement to get them out of the way. Her mom had told her to put the ones she didn't want in a box for charity. Jess had looked carefully at each book. This one? Or that one? But no, it would be like giving away a part of herself. She had to keep them all.

Jess pushed back the quilt and sat up. The window had been propped open with a wedge of wood. A faint breeze eased the stuffiness in the room and stirred the dust motes lazily where the sunlight slanted in. Sounds of chirping birds drifted in on the breeze. Jess padded barefoot to the window, pushed it open all the way and leaned out. Down below her, a sleek black cat was making his morning rounds across the backyard, leaving a trail of dark green paw prints in the dewy grass.

Jess watched as the black cat squeezed through a gap in the fence, oozing like oil into the next yard. Then she shifted her gaze higher, looking out over the rooftops directly across the Gorge to a cluster of trees with a red chimney poking up into view. Point Ellice House! Her heart gave a little skip.

Jess slid into her dressing gown and slippers. She knew, as always, her mom would be the first one up. Sure enough, her mom was sitting downstairs at the kitchen table, working on the day's list of things to do.

"Morning, Jess. Looks like it's going to be a busy day. I have to get a few groceries, make a rhubarb pie for my staff barbecue tonight, start sewing up the new curtains for your room and do some yardwork. And that's just the start."

Jess opened the fridge door. Her stomach was rumbling. She picked out a lemon poppy-seed muffin and some yogurt and set them on the table. The muffin was lemony, not too sweet, just the way she liked it.

"Mom, do you think we could go to Point Ellice House today? I could show you around."

Jess' mom sighed. "Not today, Jess. I've got too much to do. If you give me a little notice, I can schedule it in." She flipped through her planner. "Maybe the weekend after next. That might work."

"What if I help you today? I could do some of your jobs. Then maybe we could go this afternoon."

"I don't think so, Jess. It's just not going to work

17

out today. I *would* like some help though. You could go down to the store and get a few things for me. I'll write it down for you."

"Sure, Mom." Jess looked glumly at the yogurt. She didn't feel so hungry anymore. "Maybe I'll ask Dad if he wants to go with me."

"Well, you can ask him." The way she said it didn't sound very promising. "By the way, Jess, I'd like you to think about what you're going to do this summer. I don't want you moping around the house like last summer. It's about time you got involved in something. Get out of the house. Make friends. We've been here a whole year now, and it doesn't seem like you've made many friends."

Jess hoped her mom wasn't going to get started on that topic again. She was always after Jess to make friends. But it was hard to meet new people. Her stomach would start churning and she'd feel awkward and miserable. She didn't feel comfortable around new people...most people in fact. She'd rather be in her room reading a book. Her mom just didn't understand.

The stairs creaked and Jess' dad lumbered into the kitchen wearing his favourite green-and-white striped pyjamas, his hair sticking up in all directions.

"How are my two girls this morning?" He gave the top of Jess' head an affectionate pat as he went by to pour himself a cup of coffee.

"Dad? Do you think you and I could go to Point Ellice House today?"

Her dad sat down at the table and picked up the newspaper. "I'm going to work on your room today," his voice said from behind the newspaper.

Jess sighed. She knew her parents weren't interested in going to Point Ellice House. Not today and not for a good long while. But that didn't mean she couldn't go. Jess snatched up the grocery list and dashed upstairs. She dragged a comb through her hair and threw on some clothes. Then she ran back downstairs and outside.

"Bye, Mom," she called over her shoulder. "I'm going to ride over to Point Ellice House now and I'll pick up the groceries on the way home. Okay?"

"Okay, dear. Ride carefully and be back by two. That will give me enough time to make the pie," her mom called from inside the house.

Jess wheeled her bike out to the sidewalk. She glanced back at the house. It was the most rundown place on the entire block. Everything about it was off-kilter. The floors sloped so much that if you put a marble down on the floor, it would roll from one side of the room to the other. The doors didn't hang straight and the window frames were warped. Her parents were fixing it up, but so far—from the sidewalk anyway—it was hard to tell anything had been done. There were missing shingles and peeling paint. And the front steps had rotted away years ago. All that was left was a gaping hole between the ground and the veranda where long tufts of grass grew up. Her dad had rigged up a ladder to get in the front door, but usually people just went around to the back.

It must have been a nice house at one time. Maybe it was one of the houses Miss Libby had been talking about yesterday. Maybe the family that had lived here a hundred years ago—what did her mother say they were called? The Abbotts—maybe the Abbotts would have known the O'Reillys. They might have visited with each other, picnicked together, gone on boating parties up the Gorge.

Jess set off down the block. There were other old houses in the neighbourhood too. She passed one in the next block that had already been fixed up and freshly painted. There was a FOR SALE sign in the front yard. Why hadn't her parents bought one like that?

There were new houses too, square and boxy and squeezed into narrow yards. Jess knew Maxine lived in one of those houses a few blocks away. One day she'd seen Maxine getting out of a minivan parked in the driveway. Ever since then Jess had avoided that block. She didn't want to take the chance of running into Maxine if she didn't have to.

But Jess wasn't going to think about anything to do with school today. She wanted to think about what had happened at Point Ellice House. It could have been a concussion or déjà vu—something completely normal, something that could happen to anyone. And today, on such a sensible and straightforward morning, it was hard to imagine anything unusual happening at all.

She turned the corner, breezed down the hill to the bottom of the street and onto the public pathway. Her bike skimmed along the shoreline of the Gorge. The morning air was fresh and saltwater tangy against her face. Jess rode down the bike path, crossed the bridge and turned onto Pleasant Street. It had been only a matter of minutes from her house to the white picket fence of Point Ellice House.

Jess stepped into the quiet garden. Perfect. Nobody else was around to distract her. She could take all the time she wanted.

Sunlight filtered through the trees, dappling the lawn and the stands of purple foxgloves. The air was warm and still, waiting...like a breath being held. Jess felt a quiver of anticipation. The house seemed to look back at her, as if it, too, was waiting for something to happen.

A young woman was at the side veranda arranging a few wicker chairs. She was dressed in the same kind of striped and bibbed apron Miss Libby had been wearing yesterday. She greeted Jess with a warm smile, then fitted her with a tape recorder.

"Just switch it on here and it will give you a tour of the house. You're our first visitor this morning," she said. "So take your time and enjoy yourself."

Inside, Jess adjusted the headset. There was a woman's voice on the tape, crisp and clipped, with a trace of an English accent. She identified herself as the parlourmaid, and she spoke as if she was showing a new servant around the house. She chatted about the other servants and the O'Reilly family. And she explained the chores and duties to be done.

"This is the servants' entrance," the brisk voice on the tape said. "Unless Mr. or Mrs. O'Reilly say otherwise, you must enter the house only through this door. Now, wipe your feet and stand over by the sink. A great part of your day will be spent here washing dishes, peeling potatoes, and cleaning linen.

Keep it spotless. We demand everything be clean at all times. Above the sink to the left is the drying rack for dishes."

Jess paid close attention to every word. Other than the tape recording, the house was silent. The light in the room was soft as it eased through the awnings and curtained windows. The air smelt faintly of dust. And there was a trace of something sweet, a soft, whispering scent like old perfume.

Jess followed the tape-recorded tour through the scullery, the kitchen, the servery, and out into the hall past the pantry. So far she had felt nothing unusual.

Then she saw the door in the hall. It was plain and narrow. But there was something about it that made Jess stop. She turned the tape recorder off. It looked like an ordinary door, nothing remarkable about it, but still.... Then she saw the white porcelain handle turn. It moved very slowly. A pause of a heartbeat. Then the door creaked open.

Jess gasped in surprise. There, on the other side, was the girl with the fair hair—the same girl she had seen yesterday at the attic window.

"Oh! I didn't know you were there." Jess said, taking a step backwards.

But the girl did not answer. She did not even look in Jess' direction. Her face was very pale. She was dressed in period clothes like the rest of the staff at Point Ellice House. She was wearing something long and white. A dark blanket lay across her shoulders. She closed the door quietly. And then she walked right by, down the hall toward the kitchen.

Jess felt a chill in the air after she had passed. She stared after the girl. And then something else began to happen. She felt dizzy. Unsteady. The floor was shifting under her feet. Cold air crept along the back of her neck and she shivered. She was feeling quite peculiar. The hallway was becoming hazy and then....

An image of the upstairs attic appeared, quite unexpectedly, in Jess' mind. Even though she had never been upstairs, she could picture it clearly. It was dark and hot at the top of the stairs. Boxes and trunks were stacked against the walls. To the left was the maids' room—two skinny metal beds, one along each wall and not much room for anything else. The bed by the window was painted black. The other, smaller bed, was white. From the window she could see the steep pitch of the roof and a mushroom-like sprouting of red brick chimneys.

BANG! A sudden, sharp noise from the back of the house. Jess startled. Her head snapped around to see what it was. The screen door at the back, that's what it must have been. And with the noise, the image of the attic upstairs flew from her head. Snatches of voices were now drifting down the hallway. Other visitors must have arrived for the house tour.

Jess turned back toward the door. Where did the image of the attic come from? She reached out and curled her fingers around the smooth, white doorknob. But it would not turn.

It was locked.

Jess' hands were shaking as she turned the tape recorder back on and focused on the maid's voice. "Just to the right, that tiny doorway leads up to my room. No need for you to enter there today."

So! She had been right about the room.

Jess had to stop the tape again. Okay. Don't get excited. There's nothing unusual about a room in the attic. Lots of attics have rooms in them. She made herself turn the tape back on and finish the tour.

Then Jess had to return the tape recorder to the young woman in the bibbed apron. It was a perfect time to ask about the house. But her mouth turned dry and her tongue felt like a big wad of cotton batting, just the way she always felt whenever she had to talk to someone she didn't know.

"Did you like the tour?" the woman asked.

Jess nodded. Ask her. Ask her, a little nagging voice inside said.

"Do you know...?"

The woman cocked her head a little to one side, waiting for Jess to continue.

"I mean, have...have...have you ever...?" Jess could feel her hands begin to sweat. Now she wished she had never started to ask the question.

The woman was still waiting. Finally Jess' words came all in a rush. "Have you ever heard of anything strange happening here?"

"Oh. Well yes, as a matter of fact," the young woman said. "There are a lot of ghost stories about this house.

"One day, a staff member went out to cut some

flowers. When she reached out to cut the first one, she felt something on her arm. But there was nothing there. It was as if a ghostly hand had taken her by the arm and stopped her. She started to reach forward again, and the same thing happened. She was so frightened, she dropped her scissors and left. And the next day when she went back to get the scissors—what do you think she found? Laying on the grass right beside the scissors...a big bunch of flowers, already cut."

She paused and looked intently at Jess. "Many people have had strange experiences in this house—this whole area in fact. See that bridge over there?" She pointed across the lawn, through the trees and toward the very bridge Jess had cycled across earlier that morning. "Sometimes, at night, people have seen a red light weaving back and forth under the bridge. Near the water. Maybe a metre from the ground. But if they get too close.... Poof! It disappears into thin air. No one has ever been able to explain it."

Jess studied the bridge for a moment. Cars were going back and forth over it just as usual. The water was glittering below in the bright sunlight. Just a silly old ghost story—that's all it probably was.

"Well I hope you liked the tour," the woman said, picking up the tape recorder and rewinding the tape.

Jess swallowed hard. "I did. Thanks. I would have liked to have gone up to the attic though."

"The attic? Oh, no, that's not part of the tour."

"But there was a girl I saw come down the attic stairs...." Jess started to say. She was going to go on, but the young woman looked up abruptly.

25

"What girl?" she asked.

"The girl who works in the house. About my age, with long blonde hair." Jess said slowly, thinking back. There was something odd about the girl—the way she walked right by without a glance.

The young woman stared at her. There was a second of silence. The next thing she said made Jess' heart turn cold.

"We don't have anyone here like that."

3

<hr>

The Light Under the Bridge

That evening Jess waved goodbye to her mom and dad as they pulled out of the driveway and left for the staff barbecue. As soon as the car was out of sight, Jess ran back into the house. She had a plan. She'd been thinking about it ever since she'd heard about the mysterious red light under the bridge. First, she wolfed down the cold supper her mom had left for her in the fridge. Then she locked the back door and pulled her bike out of the shed.

Once again she pedalled along the Gorge pathway. Jess knew her mom and dad wouldn't want her out on her own too late, but she still had plenty of time. It was one of the longest days of the year, after all. It wouldn't be dark for hours.

She found a spot near the bridge, just off the path. A clump of bushes hid her from view if anyone should come along. She settled herself on a flat rock with a thin padding of dry, yellow grass. From here she could see the whole underside of the bridge and across the Gorge to the trees at Point Ellice House.

Time passed and nothing happened. The water rippled and glinted. One of the stubby, rainbow-coloured harbour ferries sputtered by. Two kayaks meandered lazily up the Gorge, and the evening sun slanted down and warmed her. The sounds of water lapping and the bridge traffic began to blend together. Her eyes felt heavy. She'd just close them for a minute. Then she'd....

Jess woke with a start. It was dark now. She never should have fallen asleep. She should have been home ages ago. Her mom and dad might already be home and worried about her.

Her limbs felt stiff as she jumped up. The bridge, the trees and the bushes were now merging together in the darkness like thick, woolly clumps of grey. The air was cooler and wisps of dampness rose from the water.

But just as she grabbed her bike, something caught

her eye, something moving, something small and bright. A light on the other side! A shock of light, like the first bright star in the night. And it was moving, swaying slowly back and forth as it went.

Her breath caught in her throat. Was it the ghost— the ghost from the story? Or maybe someone with a flashlight? Or even a boat? She strained her eyes. There was a definite reddish glow to it, just like in the story. Sometimes it seemed to fade a little, shrinking in size until it was almost gone. Other times it flashed bigger and brighter.

Back and forth it swayed. It seemed to be growing larger, floating across the water. It was definitely coming closer. Now it was on her side of the Gorge. It moved toward her, unhurried, closer and closer.

Her heart was fluttering like a trapped bird. She wanted to run but she was too scared to move. It wouldn't come any closer, would it? In the story the red light always vanished before anyone could get close.

But it didn't vanish. The light kept moving until it was only a few steps away. Jess could just make out a dark shape holding the light. Dark clothes. She squinted, but the brightness of the light made it impossible to see the face behind it.

Then the light flooded over Jess, focusing on her like a spotlight. The light seemed to seep under her skin and penetrate through her body. Her veins, the marrow in her bones, the backs of her eyes and even the dark corners in her mind were filled with light.

The back of her neck tingled. Then something began to happen in her mind, the beginnings of another vision, a vision like the one she had of the attic room.

Jess' own familiar world faded away—the bridge, the water, the prickly grass against her legs—it all melted into the background.

Jess relaxed her mind enough to let it happen. She did not resist. She allowed the vision to unfold. And then she was stepping out of her world, leaving it behind, and entering this strange other world....

There was a girl sitting at a piano bench. Jess could see her from the back. Her hair, the colour of golden wheat, flowed in waves down her back. She was playing the piano, a flowing, lilting song. Her body swayed as she played.

Jess could only stare. What was this? It made no sense. The girl was wearing old-fashioned clothes, a brown-and-white gingham dress and lace-up shoes. And the room was old-fashioned as well, but not one Jess had ever seen before. A front parlour, it seemed, with sofas and chairs but simply decorated. There was nothing grand about it. The piano held the commanding position in the room. Piles of music sat precariously along the top and in wobbly stacks on the floor at either side.

A woman came in through the archway from the dining room. She was short and plump with a flushed face. Her grizzled grey hair was fastened up off her neck—it looked like a big ball of dust you might find under a bed. The woman wiped her hands on her apron and sat down beside the girl on the bench. And as she did, the girl turned her head.

Jess could hardly believe her eyes. It was the same girl she had seen at Point Ellice House. Jess tried to speak, to ask what was happening. But no words came. The girl and the older woman did not seem to be aware of her. All Jess could do was watch.

"All right then, Rose," the woman said. "How about that song we were learning last night. Shall we try the second part?"

Rose played the top hand and the woman played the bottom on the well-used piano. The ivory keys were yellowed and a few stuck stubbornly. Others would no longer sound at all. The notes in the highest register were out of tune and the lowest notes set off an odd reverberating hum from deep inside the instrument. But none of this discouraged them from playing.

They were partway through the song when the front door burst open and a tall ginger-haired man in a plaid shirt and suspenders entered the room. The piano music stopped. A look of delight blossomed on Rose's face. She leapt from the piano stool and flew across the room to throw her arms around the man.

"Father! You're home! It's been such a long time." She pressed her nose into his shirt front as she hugged him.

And then Jess no longer just saw Rose. She *was* Rose. She could feel her own arms around him...smell the scent of pine cones and campfire smoke in his shirt.

"Father!..."

"Rose. It's good to see you. Those two weeks in

the bush felt like two months. Now, tell me. Have you been behaving yourself?" He kissed the top of her forehead and she could feel the tickle of his gingery moustache.

"Of course, Father."

"Is that so, Mrs. Scott?" he said, rolling a big duffel bag from off his shoulder and setting it on the floor.

The stout woman at the piano grinned and winked. "You know our Rose. Always up to something. But you should hear how her piano is coming along. As soon as she gets home from school, straight to the piano she goes and starts her practising. She hasn't missed a day since you've been gone."

Father gave Rose a squeeze. "I don't know what I would do without you, Mrs. Scott. You're like a godsend to me, looking after Rose the way you do when I am away. And on top of everything else, teaching her piano as well."

"Now, now. This old boarding house wouldn't be the same without her."

"It's more than a boarding house to us. It's our home." He'd taken off his boots and sat down on the sofa with a satisfied sigh. "...and Lord if it doesn't feel good to be home! Now tell me, how have you two been?"

"Fine, just fine, Father," said Rose, snuggling in comfortably next to him.

"And your Aunt Ellen? How is she?"

"Working hard as ever," Rose replied. "I wish she had a job where she could sit down once in a while. She works herself to the bone as a parlourmaid. She came for a visit last week. You know how she always

32

brings me something—candies or cookies—even though I tell her she should save whatever money she can? But she always does just the same. Last week she brought me a dressing comb for my birthday. Such a lovely, dark amber colour. You should see it."

At the mention of her birthday, Father rummaged in his shirt pocket and pulled out a small package. It was wrapped in white tissue and tied with ribbon. "This is for you, Rose," he said. "I've been saving it for you. And I polished it up to look its best."

Rose eagerly pulled the tissue off a black box. She opened the lid and there, nestled inside and wrapped in more tissue, was a silver locket. She picked it up by the chain and it hung, a perfect oval, turning and glinting in the light. Fine designs of flowers and leaves were painted across the enameled front.

"Oh, Father! It's beautiful!" Rose stared at it in astonishment. But how could he afford such a thing? Surely it was something a fine lady would wear.

"It was your mother's," her father said. "Now you are thirteen, I think it is time for you to have it."

Rose wrapped her arms around him and squeezed as hard as she could. "You surprised me," she said. "My birthday was last week. I wasn't expecting a gift today."

"I know, Rose. I'm sorry I missed it." He picked the locket up and held it, lovingly, in his big, calloused hands. He was silent for a moment. A sad expression flickered across his face like a shadow. "Your mother's dearest wish was to see you grow up. But she died a few days after you were born. That was all she had with you, only a few short days. How she would have loved to see you today, practically a young lady.

"Look." He opened the locket. Inside, a single word was inscribed—Courage. "Remember, Rose. No matter what trials come your way in life, your courage will get you through anything. You can always count on that."

Rose grinned. "So when you have to go back to the logging camp and we're apart again, I'll wear the locket and I'll remember, 'Courage'."

Her father clasped the chain at the back of her neck. "That is exactly right, Rose. Courage."

Rose ran to the mirror over the mantle. She turned, first one way and then the other, to see herself from both directions. The locket caught a beam of light from the window and flashed brilliantly.

"Thank you, Father," she said. "It's the best gift I've ever had. Really and truly, the best ever."

4

Disaster!

Somewhere a siren squealed, a persistent and irritating noise. The images of Rose vanished instantly, as if carried off in a puff of wind. And Jess' own familiar world shifted back into place again. It was nighttime. Jess was under the bridge. A fire engine was thundering across the bridge above her, lights flashing and siren wailing.

Had she been dreaming? Rose and Mrs. Scott at

the piano, Rose's father—had it all been a dream? It certainly didn't feel like it. It felt as real as riding her bike or going to school or having breakfast with her mom and dad.

And there was something else that was strange about the vision. At first she had felt she was just in the room watching the others. But then she had become less aware of herself. The very sense of being who she was—of being Jess—had faded way. And it felt as if she had become Rose instead. She had known exactly what Rose was thinking and feeling.

Jess shook her head and blinked her eyes a couple of times. The eerie, reddish light was nowhere to be seen. Jess hugged her arms together. They were covered in goosebumps.

What time was it anyway? She peered at her watch. After ten! She hopped on her bike, raced along the path and up the hill to her house.

Jess gave a sigh of relief. The car wasn't in the driveway after all. Her parents weren't home yet.

The next day Jess decided to go back to the bridge in broad daylight. She'd have a good look around the site where she'd had the vision. But just as she was wheeling her bike to the front of the house she heard a shout.

"Hey! It's Jess."

Jess' heart sank like a brick in water. She knew who it was, even before she looked. Maxine and Tiffany. Rats and double rats! Her footsteps quickened and she pretended she hadn't heard them.

She was just about to jump on her bike and ride away when Maxine yelled so loudly everyone on the entire block must have heard. "Jess! Wait up."

Jess had to stop then. There was no use pretending she hadn't heard them anymore. Their smiles, as they sauntered up to her, looked like phony toothpaste-ad smiles—smiles that couldn't be trusted.

"Is this where you live?" Maxine said, eyeing the house with an arched eyebrow.

Jess nodded.

"It looks like a house in a scary movie," Maxine sneered. "What's wrong with your stairs anyway?" Behind her, Tiffany giggled.

"My dad's just fixing it up," Jess tried to explain, her face turning bright red as she glanced at the pathetic-looking ladder stretched across the hole where the stairs should have been.

"He is? You could have fooled me," Maxine said. She eyed the house skeptically, and then turned to scrutinize Jess. "Where're you going?"

"Just for a ride. Nowhere special," she answered. She started wheeling her bike down the sidewalk but Maxine and Tiffany kept walking along beside her.

"Guess you'll be spending your summer with your nose stuck in a book," Maxine said.

"I...I...I haven't made any plans yet," Jess mumbled.

"Well, *we're* going to have a great summer. Aren't we, Tiffany?" Both girls nodded smugly. They reminded Jess of those toy dogs with bobbing heads that ride in the back of cars.

Jess reached the corner and turned to go down the hill. She hoped Maxine and Tiffany would leave her alone. But they kept tagging right along.

"That's not a perm in your hair, is it? It looks like it is." Maxine said. She flipped her own blonde-streaked hair behind her ears in one slick motion. "My mom once had a bad perm too. She wanted to sue the hairdresser who did it. Perms can really damage your hair, you know."

Jess gripped the handlebars so tightly her knuckles turned white. "It isn't a perm. It's just the way my hair is naturally."

Maxine stifled a snort. "Ooooo. Someone's touchy!"

Jess looked away and bit her lip instead of responding. They had almost reached the bike path at the end of the road. The last thing she wanted was to have Maxine and Tiffany follow her all the way to the bridge—to the very spot where she'd had the vision last night. Maybe she could just get on her bike and ride off. That's what she should do. Jess swung her leg over the bike.

"What's your rush?" Maxine said with a catty smile.

Jess tried to look nonchalant. "No rush."

"Thought you had nowhere in particular to go?"

"I don't."

"Hmmff. Well, we do. Tiffany's mom is driving us to the mall. So long, Je...ess." Maxine exaggerated her name when she said it, drawing it out into two syllables. The two girls turned and strolled away down the sidewalk.

Jess was glad to see them go. She pushed hard on her bike pedal and set off down the path to the foot of the bridge. Tall yellow grass and scruffy bushes of broom grew near the water's edge. There was the rock she had sat on last night. And she could see the spot—an area of flattened grass—where she had laid her bike. Jess sat down on the rock again. She checked back over her shoulder. Good. No one else was in sight. Then she turned to face the water. She could see the entire underside of the bridge and across the water to the other shoreline.

She leaned back on her elbows, stretched out her legs and waited. After a while her elbows got sore and she sat up, crossed her legs and waited some more. She was getting thirsty sitting out in the sun. Maybe she should have brought a water bottle. She checked her watch. Ten minutes to two.

Then Jess looked up, and there she was.

Rose was standing at the edge of the water on the far side of the bridge. Jess felt her heart stumble in her chest. The girl had not been there a moment ago. But now there she was, standing perfectly still in a long, white dress, gazing across the water. And even though the distance from one side of the Gorge to the other was too wide to make out her features, Jess knew it was Rose. A ghost! A real ghost! What else could she be? Jess felt a shiver like an icy cold hand passing across her skin. It was the same feeling she'd had last night under the bridge—the same feeling she'd had earlier when she'd seen Rose come down from the attic. Jess' mind started to shift. And then she was sliding...sliding headfirst...into Rose's world again.

There was a knock at the door. Mrs. Scott poked her

head into the room. Her dimpled face was red and flushed. "Are you ready, you two? It's time to go. We don't want to miss all the Victoria Day festivities."

Rose checked her reflection in the mirror. Neat and tidy. All she needed was her hat. She stretched up on her tiptoes, grabbed her best hat from the top of the wardrobe and said, "Come along, Father. Let's not keep Mrs. Scott waiting. We don't want to be late for the parade!"

She ran ahead of them, down the stairs and out onto the porch. "Hurry. The streetcar is coming. We're going to miss it!"

The streetcar rattled to a stop. It was one of the big streetcars with two platforms—one on the front and one on the back. Rose could not remember when she had seen it so full of people.

"Come on aboard," one of the passengers shouted. He was a jovial, florid-faced man. "There's still plenty of room."

Her father had caught up, but he hesitated. He looked doubtfully at the crush of people. "Thanks, but we'll wait for the next one," he called back.

"Better get this one," the man advised. "You'll miss the parade if you don't."

Rose's father stepped up onto the rear platform and pulled Rose up after him. Mrs. Scott squeezed in beside them, huffing and puffing. "My word," she gasped. "It's a good thing I'm not any bigger. There's not an inch to spare."

They perched on the very edge of the platform, grasping the railing to keep from being jostled off balance. The streetcar jerked ahead, then settled into an even rumble as it moved along the rails.

The sun was shining, hot and bright, the last day of the Victoria Day long weekend. The streetcar windows were pushed open to let in the fresh air. Despite the heat and overcrowding, the passengers were in a holiday mood—laughing and joking. Some people were even singing. A girl with white ribbons in her dark hair leaned out the window and waved to her friends on the street.

"We're going to Macaulay Point to watch the military parade," she called out.

Her friends on the street waved back. "Have fun, Lizzie."

The streetcar made a few more stops. To Rose's amazement, one or two more people managed to push their way up onto the rear platform. Now they were wedged in as tightly as books on a shelf. A couple of boys even tried to climb onto the roof of the streetcar, but the conductor caught sight of them.

"Hey, get down from there," he ordered. "Foolish boys! What do you want to do? Get yourselves killed?"

The boys jumped down and ran off, laughing.

Then the streetcar began to cross the Point Ellice Bridge. Rose held tightly to the iron railing with one hand and to her father's arm with the other. Far below them she could see the waters of the Gorge. She looked down at the locket. It glinted in the sunlight.

In the next instant—a terrible noise. The sound of splintering wood rent the air.

The streetcar shuddered and Rose's stomach lurched queasily. Then the entire streetcar plunged downward. It was only a drop of a few feet, but terrifying all the same. People gasped in alarm.

One of the men on the rear platform leapt off. "The bridge is going to go! Get off," he yelled over his shoulder as he started to run. But how could they? The streetcar was still moving forward.

Then came an even louder roar. A sound like thunder.

This time the bridge gave way completely. It collapsed beneath them, and the streetcar lurched sideways, toppling over in a sickening arch. Down. Down. They were going down. There were horrified screams and bodies hurtling against each other. Rose tried to hang on to the railing. Her muscles were straining to keep a hold. But her hand was slipping....

She drifted beneath the surface of the water. All was quiet. Her hair spread around her head like strands of seaweed. She seemed to be looking down at herself from a long distance away, as though watching another person's body in the water. Her hat...there it was, out of reach, floating farther away. Her white dress swirled gently around her, wafting in the current. Her limbs hung, completely relaxed, barely moving. She didn't try to reach the surface. She felt no urgency to breathe. She just floated.

She watched herself as if in a dream. Slowly, slowly, ever so slowly, she felt herself moving away from her body. A strange separation. A feeling of lightness. Could she be dead already? But the thought did not alarm or frighten her. In fact, it was quite the opposite. She was filled with a blissful sense of peace.

Then, just as she closed her eyes, two arms burst suddenly through the water. They shattered the stillness and seized her roughly around the waist. They were pulling her up—these two strong arms—pulling her up and up until her head broke through the surface of the water. She coughed. Water spewed out of her mouth and nose, and her breathing came in ragged gasps. She was dragged up over the side of a boat. She caught sight of the man's face, a man she did not know. Then she tumbled, heavy and sodden, into the bottom of the boat.

"You'll be all right," the stranger assured her. "The good Lord was looking out for you today."

He grasped the oars and heaved back on the handles, leaning his whole body into every stroke until the boat jarred ashore, bumping over the rocks. Two men waded into the water, lifted her out of the boat and carried her up to the grass. Her legs folded beneath her, flimsy as jellyfish, as they set her down. She turned to thank the man in the boat, but it was too late. He was already rowing away.

A lady, another person she had never seen before, came running from the big house at the top of the lawn. Her arms were full of blankets. She wrapped a thick, grey woollen blanket around Rose's shoulders.

"Stay warm, dear," she murmured into Rose's ear as she bent over her.

Rose huddled, shivering, on the grass. Where was her father? She could not see him anywhere amongst the crowd that had gathered near the water.

The bridge! She stared, wide-eyed, at the shocking sight. The entire middle span had collapsed. All that was left was a huge, gaping void. It looked like a massive skeleton brutally ripped apart, bone by bone.

And the streetcar! It lay below, half submerged in the waters of the Gorge, trapped in a clutch of twisted metal and broken timbers. People were still in the water. Their heads were bobbing, trying to keep afloat. But there was something wrong with the water. It was muddied and red. Blood! A few swimmers dove repeatedly under the surface. Were there people still trapped inside the streetcar? She didn't want to think about it.

The crowd along the water's edge grew larger. Policemen came. Firemen and doctors arrived. More rowboats were out on the water now, labouring to bring people ashore. Some of the survivors staggered weakly out of the boats, coughing, sputtering and leaning heavily on others for support. Their clothes were plastered against them, dripping streams of water and mud. They were hurriedly bundled in blankets, and hot drinks were pressed into their hands.

Other people were carried ashore, their limp bodies unresisting, limbs dangling. Rose watched in disbelief as they were laid on the ground and people clustered around, frantically trying to revive them.

One of the bodies—Rose turned her eyes away when she recognized him—was the florid-faced man who had urged them to board the streetcar. But his face was no longer red. It was greyish white, the colour of a bleak and snow-cloudy day. His eyes were open but they stared straight ahead as if frozen.

A young girl was laid down on the grass nearby. Her sodden dark hair was tied back with white ribbons. It was the girl who had called out to her friends from the streetcar window only a few minutes before. But her skin looked waxen. She did not open her eyes. She did not take a breath. Someone held a bottle of smelling salts under her nose. Surely that would revive her. But no. She did not stir. The doctor came running. He fell to his knees and tried to breathe life into her.

The girl's mother hovered, shaking and sobbing. She, too, was dripping wet. "Lizzie. Lizzie," was all she said, like a desperate prayer, over and over. The doctor sat back. He shook his head. "I'm sorry," he said. Nothing else. He put a blanket over the girl, her head covered too. The shape under the blanket was still.

Rose turned away. Where was her father? Where was Mrs. Scott? She got to her feet, her legs feeling stronger now, and clutched the blanket tightly around her shoulders as she searched frantically through the crowd. But they were not there. She ran to the edge of the water. Maybe her father was helping with the rescue. She knew he could swim. He was a big, strong, healthy man after all.

But there was still no sign of him. Her worry mounted with every passing minute. Other people fretted nearby, their shocked faces blanched white and pinched with fear. Some stared mutely. Others wept.

Where were they? Were they hurt? Were they trapped under the water? It couldn't be true. But what if it was? Rose knew she had to find them. She stumbled across the rocks, still clutching the blanket, and waded into the water.

"Father!" she cried out. Then, louder, "FATHER!"

The muddy water was up to her waist. Her clothes and the blanket clung stubbornly against her as she tried to move. She pushed the blanket aside impatiently, sank down into the water and began to swim toward the wreckage. But she had only managed a few strokes when someone grabbed her and pulled her back.

"Hold on there, young one," a man's voice warned. "You're in no condition to go back into the water. You all but drowned once already today. Best stay on the shore, where you're safe. They're doing all they can out there."

"My father...Mrs. Scott...," cried Rose. "I have to find them."

The man pulled her firmly back toward shore. His eyes were kind and steady. "There's plenty of help out there now," he said. "They'll keep at it until they find everyone. All we can do is wait."

He's right, Rose told herself. Don't be foolish. Stay calm. She paced back and forth, unable to keep still, her arms and legs trembling with fear and cold.

Another rowboat was approaching the shore. Several men waded out to drag it in, grating noisily against the rocks. Then they were lifting up the body. The head hung back, lifeless. Rose gasped when she saw the face. It was Mrs. Scott.

Mrs. Scott could not be revived. The doctor tried to make her breathe but she did not respond. All signs of life had vanished. They covered her with a sheet. It drifted down over her body like a layer of snow. And there she lay, beside a row of others—all covered, all still.

Rose hung back but she could not take her eyes off the form under the sheet. Mrs. Scott was dead. It seemed impossible. Rose would never see her smiling, round dimpled face again. They'd never sit side by side on the piano bench again. Rose blinked back the tears, feeling her throat tighten into a hard, painful knot.

"Rose?!" It was Aunt Ellen. She had been carrying an armful of blankets but she let them drop to the ground, picked up her skirts and limped awkwardly across the lawn.

"I came as soon as I heard about the accident," she said as she hugged Rose to her. "The O'Reillys asked me to bring some blankets over. I had no idea I'd find you here."

In all the confusion of the accident Rose had not given a single thought to the O'Reilly's house—she could see it now, only a few houses away—where Aunt Ellen worked as a parlourmaid.

Aunt Ellen held Rose at arm's length and surveyed her wet stringy hair and dripping clothes. "You weren't on the streetcar, were you, Rose?"

"I was. Father and Mrs. Scott...they were on it too." Rose described the accident, how Mrs. Scott's body had just been brought ashore and how they had done what they could but she had not survived. "And Father...they haven't found Father yet." The last words seemed to stick to her tongue.

Aunt Ellen held Rose to her again and slowly stroked the back of her head.

"I'm getting you all wet," said Rose. Tears and water were soaking into her aunt's apron front.

"Shhh. It doesn't matter," Aunt Ellen said. Then she began to whisper. "Please Lord. Watch over my brother. Keep him safe, dear Lord, and return him to us."

And so they stood when Rose's father was found. It was as Rose had feared—her worst fear of all. Her father was dead.

She knelt down on the ground beside her father's body. Behind her, someone was murmuring, "Such a shame...", "...hit by one of the timbers," "...didn't stand a chance."

The same woman who had draped the blanket around Rose arrived with a length of patterned fabric. "I'm sorry," she said to Aunt Ellen. "I don't have any sheets or blankets left. These are the curtains from the drawing-room."

The woman lay the fabric carefully over his body. Rose bent her head. Her tears fell onto the cloth darkening the material like a bruise. She remained at his side, unable to move. It was as if her muscles had forgotten how to move. She could barely breathe. She did not want to think about what lay under the patterned curtain fabric in front of her. No. It could not be true. She would not admit it. She could not begin to imagine life without her father.

Aunt Ellen stood by quietly, but her body was trembling and tears tracked silently down her face. She laid a hand on Rose's shoulder, "Rose, I am so sorry. He was a fine man—a dear brother to me and a wonderful, loving father to you."

Rose nodded. Her throat ached too much to speak.

Eventually—and it must have been much later as the shadows had lengthened across the lawn—Aunt Ellen said, "Maybe we should go now. I'll take you back to the O'Reilly's with me."

Rose stood up, her knees as stiff as rusty hinges. She leaned against Aunt Ellen as they crossed the lawn, staring downward. Rose's dress drooped around her, streaked with mud and torn at the hem. And that's when she noticed. Her locket was gone.

⚜

A heavy rumbling sound entered Jess' consciousness. She looked up to see a big truck passing overhead on the bridge. Jess rubbed her eyes. She was sitting on the rock near the bridge. With the sound of the truck, Rose's world had vanished as suddenly as a popped bubble. One minute it was there and the next minute it was gone.

Jess' nerves were left rattled and raw. Such a terrible accident! She could still feel herself shaking. She looked over her shoulder. What if someone had seen her during the vision? Would it have looked like she was in some kind of a trance? Would they think she was crazy? But the bushes grew thickly behind her. It was unlikely anyone had seen her at all.

Even so—a restless notion turned itself in her head. Maybe she *was* crazy. All she knew for sure was that she had to find out if Rose was real or not.

Jess wheeled her bike up to the path, then rode across the bridge and down Pleasant Street to Point Ellice House. The door of the gift shop stood open and welcoming. Jess recognized the young woman at the counter. It was the same woman who had told her the ghost stories.

"Hi there. Back again?" the young woman said cheerfully.

Jess swallowed nervously. "Uh huh. I wondered if I could ask you a few questions...about the history of the house. It's for a school project."

"Libby would probably be the best one to talk to. She's in charge and she's the one who knows more about the house than anyone. You'll find her inside. Just go through the garden and knock on the back door."

Jess' feet crunched over the gravel path, then stepped up to the back veranda. She knocked on the screen door, twisting her fingers nervously together as she waited.

She could hear footsteps tapping down the hall, then Miss Libby opened the door. Jess fixed her gaze on the silver brooch pinned to the neck of Miss Libby's blouse. She opened her mouth and the words tumbled out quickly, falling over themselves like apples spilled from a pail.

"Hello. You probably don't remember me. My name is..." she swallowed hard. "...Jess and I'm...I'm in Mrs. Marshall's class. I was here before...on a school tour. I don't want to bother you but...but...could I ask you some questions...um...for a school project?"

"Yes, I remember Mrs. Marshall's class. Would you like to come in?" Miss Libby led her into a small, crowded office near the back door and pulled up two chairs so they could sit down.

"What I wanted to ask you was...," Jess began uncertainly, and stopped. Then she began again. "Was there ever a maid who worked here? Someone called Ellen? She had a niece named Rose."

Miss Libby raised her eyebrows. "Ellen?" She shook her head. "I'm sorry. I don't know about that. The O'Reillys had a lot of servants over the years. It's possible, I suppose. Why do you ask?"

Jess looked away. What could she say? That she had visions in her head? No. That would never do. So instead she said, "I had a dream after the tour. It was a strange dream about a girl called Rose and her Aunt Ellen. After I woke up it seemed so real. I just wondered if it had really happened."

"Oh." Miss Libby gave her an understanding smile. "Sometimes dreams do seem very real."

"I'm sorry to have bothered you," said Jess, standing up. "Thank you for taking the time to talk to me."

"No problem at all, Jess. But...." Miss Libby paused. "Tell me. How did you like coming here with the class on the tour?"

"Oh, it was great! I want to find out all about this place. This is the third day in a row I've been here."

Miss Libby looked surprised. "You must really love history."

Jess nodded. "It's my favourite subject."

"Well, I have an idea. Maybe it's something that would interest you." She looked Jess up and down. "You'd be the right size, too."

"The right size for what?" Jess sat down again.

"For one of the costumes. Last summer we had a

couple of girls who volunteered here. They were about your age, I'd say. Twelve or thirteen. They wore old-fashioned costumes the way the rest of the staff here do. They usually came in the afternoons, sometimes on weekends, sometimes during the week—basically whenever they could.

"But they're not going to be around this summer, so I was wondering...." Libby looked inquiringly at Jess.

"What would they do?" asked Jess.

"All sorts of things. They'd pick raspberries from the garden. Cut flowers for the tea tables. Sometimes, if it was a hot afternoon, they'd sit in the shade of the veranda, practising needlepoint, playing checkers or painting watercolours. All the things girls might have done in Victorian times." Miss Libby paused for a second. "So, Jess, would you like to be a volunteer here this summer?"

Jess sat forward in her chair, hardly daring to believe her good fortune. "I would. I really would! I can't think of a better way to spend my summer...and...and...thank you for asking me."

"That's great, Jess. Of course you realize it is a volunteer position. I'm afraid we wouldn't be able to pay you."

Jess nodded. She had not even thought about money.

"When do you want me to start? This is the last week of school. I could start next weekend. Saturday, if you want."

"That's fine, Jess. That's just fine. I'm glad to see you're so eager to get started. Now...." She rummaged through the books and papers on the bookshelf. "Ah, here we are." She pulled out a binder. "This is the history of the place. You can borrow it and look through it, if you'd like. The more you know about the house, the more interesting you'll find it. Next Saturday, come and find me. I'll show you the dresses and you can pick whichever one you want. I think you're really going to enjoy it here, Jess."

"Thanks, Miss Libby."

"You can call me Libby."

"Okay...Libby. Thank you very, very much."

Suddenly Jess thought of something else. "Do you know if the bridge ever collapsed? A long time ago?"

"Yes. As a matter of fact it did." Libby flipped through the binder and ran her finger down one of the pages. "Here it is, the worst streetcar accident in North America. The bridge had not been maintained properly, and some of the timbers had rotted. Then one day, an overloaded streetcar was crossing, and it gave way. The streetcar fell into the Gorge and fifty-five people were killed. Ten to two in the afternoon. May 26th, 1896."

5

THE ROOM IN THE ATTIC

The last week of school zipped by as quickly as if time had been stuck in fast-forward. Now it was the first day of summer holidays and Jess' first day of being a volunteer. She sat at her dressing table, feeling her stomach twitch with nervousness as she rummaged through her box of hair clips and elastics. From way down at the bottom of the box she pulled out a white satin ribbon.

She tied her hair back with the ribbon as she reviewed the Point Ellice House binder. She'd already read the entire history from cover to cover. First she'd read the section about the accident at the bridge. 1896! More than a hundred years ago. Then she had scanned it eagerly, looking for any mention of Aunt Ellen. But there was nothing, not a single word. Finally she'd gone back to the beginning and studied it carefully, trying to memorize the important dates and facts. Peter O'Reilly bought the house in the winter of 1867. The O'Reilly family had lived in the house until 1975. It had been bought by the government and run as a museum ever since. Jess made a wry smile at herself in the mirror, as she fussed with the ribbon. All the other kids would be off to the beach or going camping, but she was still studying.

No matter how she fiddled, dark brown tendrils of curly hair kept popping out of place. Stupid hair! Why couldn't she have hair that would stay neat when she tied it back—long, wavy blonde hair like Rose? She untied the ribbon, secured her hair tightly with an elastic band and then retied the ribbon over the top. There. That looked a little better. She was ready to go.

Jess hopped on her bike and set off. The wind blew, fresh and warm, into her face. She felt almost like flying as she glided down the street. In the next block she passed the nice old house that was for sale. Only now a big orange SOLD sticker was plastered across the FOR SALE sign. Jess turned the corner and breezed down the hill.

At Point Ellice House she parked her bike against

the fence. There was no one in sight. The gate to the garden was padlocked shut and the gift shop was closed. She held her hands up to the gift shop window and peered in. There was someone there after all— the young woman who had told her about the light at the bridge. Jess knocked softly. The woman jumped; her hand flew to her throat and her eyes darted toward the window. But when she saw Jess she looked relieved, and she came, laughing, to open the door.

"Goodness! You gave me such a scare. I thought I was the only one here. When I heard you knock I thought for sure it was a ghost."

"Sorry. I didn't mean to scare you." Jess fidgeted with her hands, putting them in her pocket and then taking them out again. "I'm Jess. We talked last week."

"Yes. I remember. I'm Louisa."

"Libby said I could come and volunteer. Do you think I can wait for her in the garden?"

"Of course you can. In fact, maybe you could do me a favour. I'm going to be busy in here for a while. Would you mind opening up the house for me? Here are the keys." She handed Jess a cluster of keys on a chain. "Just remember to bring them back."

Jess stepped into the garden. It was quiet and shady. There was a soft breeze stirring the bushes, making them rustle like a skirt from long ago. It was peaceful now—no visitors, no staff carrying trays of sandwiches and teapots down to the tea garden, no noise from the recycling plant next door.

Jess could feel the heavy weight of the keys in her hand as she approached the back door. She pulled open the screen door and flipped through the labels marking the various keys. Front door, gift shop, office, attic, back door. She slipped the key in the lock, turning it all the way around. Then she pushed it open. The scullery was dark. The blind was drawn over the window, with only a slant of daylight from the open door to relieve the shadows. A damp, musty smell met her nose. She stepped inside. The floorboards creaked under her feet as she crossed the scullery and the kitchen.

What next? Jess looked down at the keys. Front door. Yes, the front door should be opened as well.

Jess tiptoed down the shadowy hallway. Then, abruptly, she stopped. There it was. The door to the attic. Jess hesitated. It wouldn't hurt if she just took a quick peek, would it?

Jess picked the key marked Attic and turned it in the lock. She heard it click. Then she closed her hand around the smooth porcelain knob and opened the door. The steps were steep and narrow, and they led straight up. Part of her wanted to close the door again and lock it up. But another part had to see what was up there. Trembling, Jess put her foot on the first stair. Then she took a deep breath and climbed, stair after stair. As she reached the top, she could see huge storage cupboards, trunks and piles of boxes crowding the walls. Thick shadows stuffed themselves into the corners. Directly across from her was a small window under the gable—the very window where Rose had been standing the first day Jess had seen her.

Jess went straight to the window and looked out. A couple of tissue-winged butterflies flitted among the flowers in the rose garden below. And she could see past the lawn to the Gorge, glittering in the morning sun. There was the bridge with its massive grey spans of metal—the site of the terrible accident that happened so many years ago. A flock of seagulls rose in unison over the water and circled in a white swirling cluster like snow in a snow globe.

Just then she saw a flash of movement—something flickering through the garden. Another butterfly? She peered through the windowpane. No, something else. The girl with the long blonde hair. Rose!

The girl emerged from the shadows of the trees into the sunlight. Her skin and hair were pale, almost translucent. Jess stared wide-eyed. There was something peculiar about the way Rose walked over the grass. Even though the grass was still covered in morning dew, her footsteps left no trace.

The air suddenly felt cooler on Jess' skin. A cold, familiar tingle crept across the back of her neck. And she knew what was about to happen....

⚜

"It's all set." Aunt Ellen sat down on the bed beside Rose. The bedsprings creaked as she settled herself. "I've just spoken to the O'Reillys, and they say we can stay here until we get ourselves sorted out. I'm so relieved. I don't abide with asking favours. It goes against my nature. But I explained about your poor father, bless his soul."

She bit her lip and glanced at Rose. "I told them it's just you and me and we have to look out for each other. Then I told them about how, with the bridge gone and all, I can't get over the Gorge and home tonight to my own room. Besides, it's too small for both of us. I'll have to find something else to rent I suppose."

Aunt Ellen was trying her best to be cheerful. "The O'Reillys are very kind. Right away they said, 'Of course, Ellen, you and your niece can use the upstairs room,' just like that. They said we could stay as long as we needed. Until we get ourselves sorted out with new arrangements.

"I've spent the night here before, now and again. A few times after some of their big fancy dinner parties when it's been too late to go home after all the washing up. And last winter when Mrs. O'Reilly had a bad spell, they asked me to stay and make hot poultices for her through the night.

"It's not such a bad room, really. It's quite comfortable. There's everything we need." Aunt Ellen rubbed her hand up and down her leg as she spoke.

"Is your leg hurting you?" Rose asked.

"Not really," she said in her matter-of-fact voice. "It just gets tired at the end of the day."

Aunt Ellen had once told Rose how she had come to have the limp. When she was a young girl, she'd taken a dare to walk across a rafter in an old barn. The rafter had broken, just like a toothpick snapping in half, and down she fell. "I don't remember actually hitting the ground," she'd said. "But I remember looking at my leg and thinking how twisted it looked, like a rag doll's." The break in her leg had taken months to heal and ever since, that leg had been an inch shorter than the other.

Aunt Ellen gave her leg a brisk pat. "Never mind.

It's nothing that keeps me from my work," she said determinedly. She always wore a serviceable black dress and kept her dark brown hair pulled back into a neat, orderly knot. Despite the limp, and although she wore no jewellery or fancy clothes, there was something very pretty about her. She had a gentle smile, straight even teeth and rosy cheeks.

Rose eyed the cramped attic bedroom doubtfully. There was barely room to walk between the two beds, but she knew better than to say so. Aunt Ellen was just doing her best after all.

"We could go back to Mrs. Scott's house," Rose suggested. "My room is quite large. There's plenty of space for both of us. It would suit us just fine." Her bedroom had a lovely big bay window that looked down over the street. It was the best room in the house, and her father had insisted she have it.

Aunt Ellen spoke slowly. "Rose, everything has changed now. Your dear Mrs. Scott is gone. She won't be there to run the boarding house or look after you either. And even if someone else took over the house...I couldn't afford to keep you there or live there myself. It's simply more than I could manage. That's the honest truth. I'm sorry Rose, but don't worry. We'll figure something out."

Aunt Ellen tried to smile bravely but the corners of her mouth trembled. "I brought up some bedding. You can have the smaller white bed. Is that all right with you? I'll have the black one. We'll hang our things in the closet. It will be good and cozy here for the time being. You'll see."

Aunt Ellen took a folded sheet, snapped it open,

laid it smoothly over the mattress and tucked it in. Rose shook the pillow down into the crisp, white pillowslip and tucked it under the cover. How smooth and inviting it looked. Suddenly she felt completely exhausted by everything that had happened. She was too tired to talk or listen or even think anymore.

"I'm sorry, Aunt Ellen. I think I'm going to have to go to bed now."

"That's right, dear. You have a good sleep."

Rose unbuttoned her dress and hung it in the closet. Then she slipped between the covers, wearing her petticoat in place of a nightgown—the rest of her clothes were still at Mrs. Scott's. But Rose was too tired to mind.

"Goodnight," she murmured, and closed her eyes.

It was morning now and Rose heard Aunt Ellen stirring. "I'm going downstairs to start work," she whispered. "Come down when you're ready, and I'll fix some breakfast for you."

Rose heard her footsteps going downstairs. She lay for a moment, partway between dreaming and awake. A heavy sadness sat waiting on the edge of this warm half-sleep. For a few moments she couldn't think what it was. Then, with a jolt, it all came back to her—the accident, her father and Mrs. Scott both dead. Tears flooded her eyes, spilled hotly on her cheeks and soaked her pillow. She sobbed, her shoulders shaking and her stomach muscles tight and aching. Then gradually her sobs subsided and, except for the occasional sniffle, she lay, staring miserably at the wall.

Finally she made herself sit at the side of the bed. Then, summoning all her resolve, she went to the washstand and poured water from the white ceramic jug into the bowl. The water felt cool on her burning eyelids and cheeks. She unplaited her braid and eased a comb through the hair until it was smooth. Then she tied her hair back, bending to peer into the mirror at her puffy, red eyes.

She took her white muslin dress from the closet. There was a mud stain on the skirt and a tear at the hem. It drooped sadly on the hanger, the rows of pleats down the front no longer starched and ironed perfectly straight as they had been the morning before. How long ago it seemed! So much had changed in one day. She pulled the dress over her head and smoothed it down the best she could.

People would expect her to be wearing mourning clothes—clothes that were somber and dark out of respect for the dead. A black ribbon would have done, at the very least. But she didn't even have a black ribbon.

She straightened the bedcover, went downstairs and out the side door into the fresh, glistening morning. Dew lay heavily, whitening the lawn like a glaze over a pudding. The servant's toilet was outside. Aunt Ellen had pointed out the door yesterday, tucked discretely in the corner of the back veranda. "We come outside to this toilet. We don't use the bathroom inside. That one is only for the O'Reilly family," she'd explained.

When Rose came, shivering, back into the house

and down the hall into the kitchen, Aunt Ellen handed her a plate with hot, buttered toast and apricot jam.

"Did you sleep alright?" Aunt Ellen asked. She was making a determined effort to smile brightly, but her eyes were reddened just as Rose's were.

"Yes. Did you?"

"Quite well."

The Chinese cook and the houseboy both hung back, taking shy sidelong glances in their direction.

"This is Moon, our cook," Aunt Ellen said. He had a pigtail halfway down his back and his white shirt hung loosely over black pants. On his feet he wore black cotton slippers.

Moon nodded his head in greeting, keeping his eyes cast respectfully downward.

"He speaks only a few words of English," Aunt Ellen said. "But he understands most of what you say." She turned to the houseboy. "And this is Sing."

The houseboy stepped forward. He was a smaller version of Moon, pigtailed and dressed in similar clothing. The top of his head was even with the top of Rose's, and his eyes were as dark as licorice.

"Rose is going to be staying with me upstairs for a while, Sing. You can show her around the garden today. Maybe she can help you with your chores."

At that moment the bright sound of a bell rang out.

"That will be Mrs. O'Reilly," Aunt Ellen said. "She'll be finished with her breakfast, I expect. Come along, Rose, and I'll introduce you to her."

Rose brushed the crumbs off her dress and followed Aunt Ellen down the hall, around the corner and into a room lined with books. Mrs. O'Reilly sat with her breakfast things spread neatly on a table in front of her. She had white hair and a gently aged face, and she wore a dark plum-coloured dress. Rose could see the material had a sheen to it. Silk. Imagine wearing a silk dress at breakfast time!

Aunt Ellen bobbed a curtsy. "I beg your pardon, ma'am. I'd like to present my niece, Rose."

Rose hoped Mrs. O'Reilly would not notice the mud stains and the ripped hem of her dress.

But Mrs. O'Reilly had a kind smile. "Well, child. So you are Rose. I am sorry to hear about your father. It was a terrible tragedy."

"Yes, ma'am."

"I hope you will be comfortable here until you get yourself settled. How fortunate that we have the upstairs room. It has proven itself useful every now and then."

"I'm grateful for your kindness, ma'am," Rose said. She tried her best to appear well-mannered and to do and say all the right things.

"You are most welcome, my dear," said Mrs. O'Reilly. She folded her napkin and placed it on the table. "I've finished with my breakfast now, Ellen. Thank you."

As Aunt Ellen began arranging the dishes and the teapot on a tray, they heard the front door open. A distinguished man with a full white beard, a silver-buttoned waistcoat and a gleaming watch-chain, came striding into the room.

"Peter, this is Rose, Ellen's niece," said Mrs. O'Reilly.

"Aah, Rose. Of course. Lovely to meet you, young Rose." Mr. O'Reilly shook her hand firmly. His eyes smiled into hers.

"Thank you, sir."

"I hope you'll make yourself at home. Now, Ellen...," he rubbed his hands together. "I could do with some good, hot tea."

"Very well, sir. Come along, Rose." Aunt Ellen carried the tray carefully so the dishes wouldn't rattle, and Rose followed her back down the hall.

"Normally you mustn't go beyond this door." Aunt Ellen nodded toward the door in the hallway covered in red baize fabric, as they passed through. "It divides the house into two parts—the servants' side and the O'Reilly's side. There are a few other rules you should know about as well. No running in the house and no loud noises. You can remember that, can't you, Rose? You must be as quiet as a church mouse."

"Don't worry," Rose replied. "I'll tiptoe everywhere and I'll only speak in whispers." The day before she had learned that she must only enter the house through the scullery door off the back veranda. She could not use the the main entrance doors or the veranda on the other side of the house. Those were only for the O'Reillys and their guests.

So many rules! At Mrs. Scott's house she could go upstairs or downstairs, through the front door or the back. And she could sit on any veranda she pleased. Still, she felt fortunate the O'Reillys were kind enough to offer her a place to stay.

"Have I met everyone in the house now?" Rose asked. Until that moment she had not given much thought to the family that lived there.

"Not quite. There's Miss Kathleen, the daughter...."

"Would she be about my age?"

"No, she's a few years older than me, but still quite a young woman. She's not up yet this morning. She was out late last night. She'll ring her bell when she's ready for her breakfast." Aunt Ellen glanced up at the row of bells over the doorway, as they entered the servery. "There's a bell for each room, so I know who's calling. You'll get to recognize the different sounds they make.

"And there are Miss Kathleen's two brothers, Master Frank and Master Jack. They are both grown men. We passed their rooms just back in the hallway. Master Frank has been away for quite some time, working in the interior of British Columbia. The Kootenays, I believe. So you won't meet him.

"And then there's Master Jack, the younger brother. He's already had his breakfast and gone into town. He works in an office downtown. He's a great sportsman, Jack is. Tennis, croquet...name any kind of sport and he plays it."

Aunt Ellen set the tray down on the counter. "Now I've got work to do, Rose. Why don't you find Sing? He'll be outside now doing his chores, I expect. See what you can do to help him out. Perhaps he'll show you how to feed some of the animals, and you can take that over from him. That way, you'll feel you're earning your keep."

Rose could see Sing through the screen at the back door. He was carrying a pail away from the house. She crossed the veranda in two big steps and her feet crunched along the gravel path as she hurried after him. She finally caught up to him at the pigpen, just as he dumped the pail of kitchen scraps over the fence and into the pen. He turned and smiled a shy greeting.

"I'll help you, Sing. Can you show me what to do?"

The pig was snorting greedily and pushing the food through the mud with his snout. Its body was a tremendous size, dirty white with big grey splotches and a bristling of coarse hair. There was something that looked almost human about the animal. It lifted its head and looked at her with small pink eyes, then grunted loudly and went back to rummaging through its food.

"Daisy," Sing said.

"Daisy? Is that the pig's name? How would it be if I fed Daisy every morning? That will be one less chore for you. You probably have more than enough to do."

Sing nodded. "Thank you." He stole a quick and mischievous glance in her direction. "Rose and Daisy. They be flowers. Not girl. Not animal."

Rose looked at him, puzzled.

"You be flower girl." He poked a finger into her arm and there was a twinkle in his eyes. "And it be flower pig," he added, turning to point at the pig.

Rose laughed and the noise sounded strange to her ears. Only this morning she thought she'd never laugh again. But now, all the events from yesterday came rushing back, and the laughter quickly dried up in her throat.

And as Rose returned to the house, she looked up through the trees. Her heart skipped a beat. For there, grim and looming, was the huge, broken bridge. It was impossible to ignore its presence. As long as she stayed at the O'Reillys' house, she would be living in the shadow of the bridge.

She walked to the edge of the bank and was surprised to see that even now there were still masses of boats swarming the water. Divers bobbed up and down like slick-headed seals. A tall derrick had now been brought in and positioned to haul up the wreckage. There were huge timbers submerged in the water and there was the streetcar itself, smashed like a child's toy.

"Rose?"

Rose turned. It was Sing. "We pull rhubarb now?" he suggested, his eyebrows raised.

She nodded and followed him into the kitchen garden, grateful to have something to take her mind off the accident. The sun warmed their backs as they bent down and snapped the tender, young stalks close to the ground. Then, just as they were each gathering up an armful of rhubarb, a tall, angular man with a shovel came marching across the lawn toward them.

"Mr. Norman. Gardener," Sing said to Rose under his breath. He took a step backwards.

The man walked straight up to Sing. His mouth scowled, dark, like a slash of ink. His hat shadowed his eyes.

"China boy! You were supposed to dig up the far corner so I could plant the lettuce. Well—" He jerked his head toward the other side of the garden, "does that look dug up to you?"

"Sorry. Very sorry," Sing mumbled.

The gardener swung the shovel. It sliced into the dirt, only a few inches from Sing's feet. "There's the shovel. I suggest you get busy with it. I'm planning to plant this afternoon and it better be done by then. I've just about had enough of you. I don't know whether to call you stupid or just plain lazy."

"He is not stupid. And he's not lazy either," Rose cried out. "He's been working hard doing chores."

Mr. Norman turned slowly and fixed Rose with a hard, flinty stare. "And who are you?"

"Rose." She met his stare directly.

"What do you think you're doing here?"

"I'm helping Sing."

"Mmph," he snorted. "I can't abide young upstarts, especially in my garden. You'd best remember that." He pressed his thin lips together and spat on the ground. Then he turned and stomped away.

Rose was as shocked as if he had slapped her across the face. She stared after him. He had no right to treat them that way. What was wrong with the man?

6

A YOUNG LADY IN THE HOUSE

Sing grabbed the rhubarb and scuttled back to the kitchen like a crab running for cover under a rock. Rose had to hurry to keep up with him. He wiped his feet briskly on the doormat and pushed open the screen door. Moon stopped stirring the bubbling pot on the massive black stove just long enough to inspect the rhubarb. He said something in Chinese and returned to his stirring.

Sing rinsed the rhubarb in the sink, then lined it up on the chopping board and began slicing it into knuckle-sized chunks. *Chop. Chop. Chop.*

Rose stood watching the knife rise and fall but Sing did not look in her direction. She knew he was hurrying to finish off the rhubarb so he could get back to the garden and start digging.

Finally she could keep quiet no longer. "Is the gardener always so mean?" she asked.

Sing shrugged but he did not reply. The sparkle had gone from his eyes.

Ting-ting, ting-ting. The jangle of a bell made Rose jump just as if she'd been poked with a pin. A moment later Aunt Ellen came bustling into the kitchen.

"Oh, Rose, there you are. Good. That was Miss Kathleen's bell. She's awake now. I can take you in to meet her."

Aunt Ellen led the way down the hall, past the red baize door and around the corner to Miss Kathleen's room. The young woman was stretched out on a reclining couch. Her hair was down past her shoulders, and she wore a blue velvet robe over her nightdress. On her feet were matching blue quilted slippers.

"Good morning, Ellen." Her eyes went from Aunt Ellen to Rose. "This must be your niece."

"Yes she is. I'd like you to meet Rose," Aunt Ellen said.

"Please, do come and sit down, Rose. We'll have a visit and get to know one another," suggested Miss Kathleen.

Rose sat down on the edge of a chair and tried to tuck the stained part of her skirt out of sight.

"Ellen," Miss Kathleen said. "Will you take my tan

shoes and give them a good polish? I want to wear them this afternoon to the Pembertons' garden party."

When Aunt Ellen opened the wardrobe door, Rose had to stop herself from gasping. She had never seen such a crowd of lovely dresses. And all for one person. What luxury! Her eyes feasted on all the fabrics and colours. How she would love to touch the various materials and take each dress out to admire it from every side. Aunt Ellen took the shoes from the bottom of the wardrobe and closed the door, concealing the dresses once again.

"Thank you, Ellen. I'll ring the bell when I'm ready for my tea."

Aunt Ellen nodded and took the shoes out of the room. Then Miss Kathleen turned to Rose. "What a lovely name you have. I do so love roses. I think they may very well be my favourite flower. Have you seen our garden yet? We have some new rose varieties this year. I chose them myself. They're going to be exceptionally good, I think."

Miss Kathleen chatted away easily. Rose tried to be polite, nodding and making suitable replies the best she could, but all the while she was admiring the beautifully decorated room. There were pretty ornaments on the mantel, a thick carpet under her feet, lovely pictures and a bookshelf stuffed with books. And on a shelf in the corner of the room, there was a porcelain pig, so tiny it could have easily fit in the palm of her hand.

"Oh! It's Daisy," Rose exclaimed aloud, then clapped her hand over her mouth. She hadn't meant to speak out of turn. But it did look exactly like Daisy.

She could see the distinguishing grey splotches, even from where she was sitting.

Miss Kathleen looked surprised. "You've met Daisy already then?"

"Yes. This morning with Sing. He showed me how to feed her kitchen scraps." Rose stopped and bit her tongue. Perhaps "kitchen scraps" was not a suitable topic for conversation with a lady.

But Miss Kathleen did not seem to mind at all. "Daisy does have a tremendous appetite, doesn't she? Well, that little porcelain pig on the shelf was a present from my father. He couldn't resist buying it for me. It does bear a remarkable likeness to our Daisy.

"Do you know, Rose? I think it will be very nice having another young lady in the house." Miss Kathleen rang the bell. Aunt Ellen appeared a few minutes later, carrying the tan shoes.

"Thank you, Ellen. I'll have my tea now. And thank you, Rose, for the visit. I've enjoyed meeting you."

As soon as they were back in the kitchen, Aunt Ellen said, "And what did you think of Miss Kathleen?"

"I liked her very much indeed. She said it would be nice to have a young lady in the house."

Rose watched Aunt Ellen's rough and red-knuckled hands as she got the tea ready. They were hands made for heavy work, hands that had seen years of scouring pots and scrubbing floors. Each fingernail was cut straight across, squared off in a no-nonsense fashion. How different they were from Miss Kathleen's smooth, white hands, tapering to perfect oval-shaped nails.

"Maybe our luck will turn," Aunt Ellen was saying. "Suppose a little money came our way. Do you know what I would do? I'd get myself one of those treadle sewing machines and start my own business designing dresses. I'd use only the best materials and I'd finish them with lovely trims. Yes," she nodded to herself, "I could sit down and it would be much easier on my leg. I would think a seamstress's salary would match a maid's, perhaps more if you were a hard worker and clever at it."

Rose closed her eyes for a moment. Imagine not having to work at all. Just think what it would be like to live the life of a lady—to have a room full of beautiful things, fine clothes to wear, servants to clean your shoes and make your tea, and invitations to fancy parties? A life of comfort and privilege. And no cares or troubles at all.

Rose was standing with Aunt Ellen on the porch of Mrs. Scott's boarding house as the next-door neighbour opened the door.

"I appreciate your kindness," Aunt Ellen said. "We've been wanting to come around and collect Rose's belongings for a few days now. I've had to ask the O'Reillys for a little extra time off this week. There are so many things we have to attend to. They said I could have two afternoons. Wasn't that generous? Usually I get two afternoons off in a month."

The neighbour stepped back from the door and let them in. "All the other boarders have packed up and moved out. It's a good thing Mrs. Scott gave me an extra key." She shook her head. "Such a tragedy. They're saying it's the worst streetcar accident in North

America. Fifty-five people dead. Imagine! And twenty-seven seriously injured. Who would have thought such a thing could happen here in Victoria? And poor Mrs. Scott, may she rest in peace, it's not going to be the same without her. The house has been so quiet, the curtains closed, no one coming or going. It won't be long before it's sold, I suppose."

Rose felt strange being back in the house again. It seemed both familiar and unfamiliar at the same time. There was the piano and the piles of music ready, as always, to topple over. There was the long dining table where she had shared so many suppers with the boarders. But now a fine layer of dust covered the furniture, and the rooms were silent and still.

Rose went upstairs to her father's room. It was cramped and dark, but in all the years he had lived there, he never considered taking one of the larger rooms. "This suits me fine," he always used to say whenever Rose would bring the subject up. He did not have many things—just a few books and clothes. She touched the sleeve of one of his shirts hanging in the wardrobe, then pulled it toward her, pressing her face into the cool fabric. It still smelt faintly of pine cones and campfires. And it reminded her of the tickle of his moustache when he kissed the top of her forehead.

All his belongings fit neatly into a single box, and, an hour later, Rose slid the box under her bed in the attic room at the O'Reillys' house. She would sleep better knowing his things were there.

Neither did her own possessions amount to much: an armful of books and a handful of hair ribbons, the amber comb Aunt Ellen had given her for her birthday, a straw hat (not her best. *That* one had been lost in the accident), a wool coat with sleeves that didn't quite reach her wrists, nightgowns, stockings and underwear, a few pinafores and two dresses. That was the lot.

She hung the brown-and-white gingham dress in the narrow closet. The second dress was dark grey with black buttons down the front. She would wear it this afternoon. But how she dreaded the thought. There were to be two funerals—Mrs. Scott's and her father's. Rose's fingers felt thick and clumsy as she tried to make the buttons go into the holes. She fumbled with her shoelaces, and she kept dropping the comb as she fixed her hair.

During the services, Rose twisted a handkerchief around her fingers so tightly it hurt. The minister droned through the prayers and Bible readings, but Rose's mind refused to pay attention. It was as if he spoke another language. She had no idea what he was saying. It did not seem possible that her father and Mrs. Scott were actually dead.

Aunt Ellen sat next to her, dabbing at her eyes with a soggy handkerchief.

Afterwards, people spoke to them in hushed voices. One or two of the ladies kissed her on the cheek—light, fluttering kisses that felt like brushes from a butterfly's wing. They meant to be kind. Rose knew that. But still, all the words, prayers and butterfly kisses in the world would do nothing to close the wretched hole she felt in the pit of her stomach.

Aunt Ellen stopped in front of the massive door of a

downtown office building.

"This is it," she said. She ran a hand over her hair to make sure it was tidy and gave Rose a nervous smile. Then they opened the door and climbed up a long flight of marble stairs to a door marked, Bradshaw & Harrop, Barristers and Solicitors.

Mr. Bradshaw appraised their plain clothes with a cold, practised glance and indicated with an outstretched hand that they might sit down. His eye took in Aunt Ellen's limp as she crossed the room.

The lawyer sat on the far side of a broad, gleaming desk. He put his glasses on the end of his nose and studied the papers in front of him for a few moments. Then he looked over the top of his glasses and fixed his eye on Aunt Ellen, "I have reviewed the will and everything appears to be in order. But I regret to say the estate does not amount to much. There is very little in the way of money or assets. And there are the funeral expenses and legal costs to consider as well, of course." He cleared his throat noisily at this point. "What little remains will be put into a trust account. You are the legal guardian to your niece. You can draw upon the account on her behalf until she reaches the age of twenty-one."

He took off his glasses and his expression softened slightly. "Simply put, you can withdraw money for your niece when she needs it. That is the intent, but, to be frank, I expect it will not be enough to keep her more than a few months. I'm sorry that I do not have happier news."

Rose blinked in surprise. Only enough money to last a few months? How could there be so little to show for her father's hard work? He must have spent his money to keep her comfortable and cared for in the big room with the bay window at Mrs. Scott's. There would be no money now to help her and Aunt Ellen get re-established. Not even enough money to buy Aunt Ellen a sewing machine.

Aunt Ellen's face was pale as she stood up, shook Mr. Bradshaw's hand and thanked him for his time.

The lawyer shook Rose's hand next and said. "I'm sorry circumstances aren't any better. Good luck to you both." He sat down again, instead of seeing them to the door.

"Don't worry, Rose." Aunt Ellen said as they went down the stairs. "I'm sure we'll manage somehow."

As soon as Rose returned to the O'Reillys'—oh, how strong the impulse!—she wanted to rush to the piano. When she had lived at Mrs. Scott's, music always helped her feel better, especially when she was upset. And today the urge to play was so strong, her fingers tingled. If only she could play one of the O'Reillys' pianos. She'd seen one in the drawing-room and one in the dining room. But she knew the rules. Do not go past the red baize door. No running. No noise. Be as quiet as a church mouse. Aunt Ellen had made it clear; they mustn't infringe on the O'Reillys' kindness.

So, instead, she slipped away to the bottom of the sloping lawn, down the path to the water. She wandered along the shoreline, past the boathouse, toward the bridge. And as she went, she scanned the beach, searching for something glinting in the light. Searching for her locket.

7

THE LADY IN BLACK

"Jess. Jess?"

Someone was calling her name. It felt as if she was being dragged out of a deep sleep. Jess made herself refocus. She was looking out the attic window at Point Ellice House. It was her first day of volunteering, and someone—Libby or Louisa—was downstairs looking for her.

But Jess didn't want to be found up here. She

scurried back across the attic floor. There was Rose's bedroom off to the side. She saw it now—just a glimpse of a whitewashed wall through the partly opened door. But there was no time to stop. Quickly she ran down the stairs, closed the door and locked it behind her. She could hear the voice still calling her name from the far end of the house. Jess pushed a stray strand of hair back behind her ears, grabbing a hasty moment to catch her breath.

How long had she been up in the attic? It felt like hours had passed. And during that time she'd seen at least a week of Rose's life. But why was Rose contacting her—making her see into the past? What could Rose want with her?

Jess hurried down the hall. Libby was at the office door.

"Jess! There you are. I was wondering where you got to." Libby gave her a curious look.

"Louisa asked me to open up the house...." Jess began and then trailed off. She'd better say something else. "And then I was just trying to study some of the facts from the binder you lent me. I've got a lot of it memorized."

"Memorized!" Libby looked impressed. "That's wonderful, Jess. Well, let's get you started then. How about picking out your costume?"

Libby went into the office and took two outfits down from the hook on the wall. "Which one do you like?" she asked, holding them both up.

The first was a simple long skirt and white blouse, and the other one was prettier and more elaborate. Immediately Jess' eyes were drawn to the second dress. It was a soft shade of forget-me-not blue with flounces on the skirt.

Normally Jess would have picked the plainer one. She liked to wear the most ordinary and unassuming clothes she could find—clothes that wouldn't draw attention to herself. But now she hesitated, looking back and forth between the two costumes.

"The blue one," she said, feeling deliciously daring.

When she slipped the blue dress over her head and shook the flounces down into place, Libby clapped her hands. "Jess! You look like you've just stepped out of an old-fashioned picture."

Jess turned in front of the mirror, checking herself from all sides. It was true. She did look like someone from an old-fashioned picture, someone she hardly recognized. The dress fit her perfectly, swirling gracefully at her ankles as she moved. She looked like a different person—someone with confidence, someone self-assured.

Libby had a number of jobs for Jess over the following days and somehow—maybe because of the the forget-me-not blue dress—Jess managed each job as easily as if she'd been doing it for years. Libby was pleased with how she was fitting in. So was Jess. She greeted guests at the door and told them some of the history of the house (not that it didn't make her nervous, but there was something exciting about it as well). She learned to play croquet and helped visitors with the rules of the game. She picked flowers from the garden and arranged them in vases. She did pencil sketches, and, on hot afternoons, she sat on the shady veranda and made lavender sachets. The days passed pleasantly, and Jess was enjoying herself more than she had for a long, long time.

Being at Point Ellice House was almost like living in another time. But not just any time—Rose's time. Rose would have lifted her skirts to climb the stairs, just as Jess did. Rose, too, would have picked raspberries in the garden. And her feet would have crunched down the very same gravel paths.

Jess was thinking about this one day as she carried a box of jam jars down the path. Libby had asked her to stick labels on jars of strawberry jam for the gift shop. It was so hot inside, Jess had decided to go outside.

A few weeks of summer had already come and gone. There had been no more visions since her very first morning of volunteering. Rose had seemed so anxious to contact her then. As if there was something important she wanted Jess to know. But after that first morning in the attic, there always had been other people around. Maybe that was why there had been no more visions. Jess would have to find a place where she could be alone. And not only that, it should be a place that had been important to Rose. The garden! The garden was where Rose and Sing had cut rhubarb.

Jess shifted the heavy box, stepped off the path and crossed the lawn to a shady part of the yard near the fence. She settled herself down on the grass and looked around. Perfect. Nice and cool. She could see the kitchen garden and nobody else was around.

She began sticking the gold Point Ellice House labels onto the jars, making sure each one was centred and straight. She was down to the last jar, and still nothing unusual had happened. Everything felt as it usually did, as normal as could be. But then, as she was reaching for the last label, a sudden cool breeze snatched it away from her fingers and blew it, scurrying, across the lawn. Jess jumped to her feet and chased the wind-dashed label to the farthest corner of the yard. There it was, snagged in the dense bushes. And just as she was fishing it out from a tangle of leaves, quite suddenly it happened. She could feel Rose's presence. She could not actually see her, but she knew, without a doubt, that Rose was there. A shiver passed down her back. The greenery of the garden began to melt away. And she was slipping back into Rose's world again.

There was a knock at the screen door. Rose put down her pen and looked up from her notebook. She had spent the last few hours trying to catch up with school assignments—composition, geography, mathematics—and she was glad of the diversion. She could see the outline of a tall, lanky boy through the screen door. He stepped back as she opened it, swept his cap off and held it in front of his chest with both hands.

"I'm the rag boy, miss. Do you got any rags or scrap you want hauled away? Or knives for sharpening?" He spoke in a mumble and looked down even when he spoke. His clothes were dirty and tattered, and a smudge of soot darkened one cheek.

"I'm not sure. I'll have to ask," Rose said.

She noticed as she turned, that his gaze shifted toward the kitchen and he took a deep breath, savouring the smell of the hot, almond shortbreads that had just come out of the oven.

Rose found Aunt Ellen in the dining room, arranging sprays of mock orange blossoms in a vase. The flowers looked pretty with their snowy petals and delicate scent but it seemed a shame to Rose that they should be cut. She always thought flowers were best left in the garden where they would last. But she would never say as much. She knew the O'Reillys liked to keep cut flowers in almost every room of the house.

"The rag boy's here, Aunt Ellen. What should I tell him?"

"Oh, that boy again," Aunt Ellen said. "He came by last week. I suppose he could sharpen the kitchen shears. You can give him this for his trouble." She dug in her apron pocket and handed Rose a penny. "Here...and you take this one for yourself." She pulled another penny from her pocket.

Rose began to protest but Aunt Ellen pressed it into her hand. "Get yourself some candies with that. We're not so badly off that you can't have a little sweet once in a while. Go on then. Don't keep the rag boy waiting."

Rose put both pennies in the pocket of her pinafore, thinking of gumdrops, lemon drops and caramels. She felt her mouth water as she pulled the heavy shears down from the shelf. Their powerful blades were long, longer than the length of her hand,

and tapered to a point.

"Can you sharpen these?" she asked the rag boy.

"I reckon so."

Rose followed him out to the road where an old cart and horse stood. The horse's back swayed and the weight of its head seemed to drag the neck down. Its coat was dull brown and the cast of its eye was cloudy.

The rag boy crawled into the back of the cart and rummaged through the rotting wood, scrap metal and heaps of rags. Finally, from somewhere under the pile, he pulled out a pumice stone. He spat on the stone and set to work sharpening the blades. *Scrape, scrape, scrape*—a steady, even rhythm. The light glinted brightly on the blades when he handed them back to her.

"You did a good job," she said and gave him a penny. For one guilty moment, she thought about giving him the second penny. He probably needed it more than she did.

"Thank you, miss." He pocketed the penny with a quick motion. Rose noticed his jacket sleeve ride up his arm, revealing a thin, bony wrist.

Rose hesitated for a moment but she couldn't stop herself from saying, "Forgive me for asking, but do you get enough work to live on? Properly, I mean. Enough for food and a place to live?"

The rag boy's dark eyes shifted away. His only answer was a shrug of his shoulders.

"And the rest of your family? Your parents...?"

"Don't got none, miss. I work for Mr. Bagley. He lets me use his cart and horse as long as I mind them.

And he lets me sleep in the barn over the horse stall."
The rag boy shifted his feet.

Rose saw then how the boy's shoe had split along
the side where the leather met the sole. The second
penny felt like it was burning a hole through her
pocket. She could stand it no longer. "Please...take
another penny," she said. "I want you to have it."

But the rag boy would not accept it. "Sharpening
scissors is one penny, miss, not two. That's the fair
price."

Then Rose had a sudden idea. "Wait right there,"
she said, and she ran back into the house. The rows
of almond cookies lay cooling on the counter. Sing,
who had been sweeping up the crumbs from the
floor, watched in amazement as Rose scooped six or
eight cookies into a tea cloth, then turned to him
with a warning finger pressed to her lips.

"Shhhh. Don't breathe a word."

Sing offered no objection and the trace of a smile
flickered across his face. Rose ran out again, banging
the screen door behind her.

"Here," she said, panting heavily and pressing the
cloth into the rag boy's hands. "Will you take these?"

He looked surprised as he opened the cloth and
the warm, wonderful smell met his nose. "Thank you,
miss." He eagerly took a cookie and popped the entire
thing into his mouth. He chewed it quickly and then
took another. Rose watched with satisfaction as he ate.

The clouds overhead had darkened and the wind
was picking up, rippling through the hay in the field
across the road like waves on a blustery, yellow-green
sea. And, all along the fence, a row of tree saplings

strained against their ties like boats pulling at their moorings.

The rag boy pocketed the remaining cookies, pulled his jacket tighter around him and scanned the threatening sky. He had just climbed back into his cart, when a fine carriage came rattling down the road. It stopped directly in front of them. The horse that drew the carriage was magnificent, towering over them and pawing the ground like a race horse. Its powerful muscles rippled under its black, gleaming coat, and bellows of air rushed in and out of its flared nostrils. The eyes flashed, the neck arched arrogantly and there was a disdainful twitch of the tail.

Behind the fine horse, high in the carriage, sat a boy of about twelve years, in a smart, brown corduroy suit. An older girl with bouncy blonde ringlets sat next to him. The green velvet of her dress and the ribbons on her fancy hat matched exactly. When she looked down, she wrinkled her nose, the same way a person might react to cow manure.

With her parasol, she tapped the man sitting in front of her in the driver's seat. "I'll deal with this, driver." Her voice was thin and high-pitched.

Then she turned to address the rag boy. "Your silly old rubbish cart is taking up the entire road. Move to the side at once and let us pass."

The rag boy inclined his head toward Rose and touched a finger to his cap. Then he flicked the reins, and the old horse slowly and deliberately set one foot in front of the other, dragging the creaking rubbish cart away.

The magnificent black horse pranced by with

clattering hooves. As the carriage passed, the ringletted girl said out of the side of her mouth—but loud enough for Rose to hear—"Street urchin."

The carriage turned the corner and rattled out of sight. Behind the carriage, a spattering of gritty dust blew into Rose's face. She squeezed her eyes shut and turned away, coughing. Her eyes stung, partly from the dust and partly from the insult.

Rose was brushing the dirt off her skirt as Aunt Ellen came out to the roadside.

"How did he do with the shears?"

Rose handed the gleaming shears back to Aunt Ellen. "Sharp as razors," she said. "Aunt Ellen, did you see those people who just passed by in the fancy carriage? Do you know who they are?"

"That was Cynthia Abbott and her brother Francis. They live on the other side of the Gorge, across the water. I know their parlourmaid, Mavis. From what she tells me, they're a bit of a handful, those two."

Rose pressed her lips together. Especially that Cynthia! she wanted to say. Sour as a pickle in her fancy pickle green dress and matching hat.

Aunt Ellen dropped into the kitchen chair with an exasperated sigh. "It's impossible! I'm sure I've looked at every boarding house in the city this afternoon. Anything that's worth looking at is far too expensive, and the rest are just not suitable. Rats, filth, horrid smells. You have no idea. I even went around to my old boarding house in Esquimalt. I know it's small but at least it was clean. I was hoping I could get my room back again, but it's already been rented. They had no rooms left at all." She sighed again and then squared her shoulders in a determined fashion. "I'll have another go at it when I get my next afternoon off. Goodness, it's hot today."

She went to the sink and held a cold, wet cloth first against her forehead and then against the back of her neck. "The O'Reillys will be wanting lemonade. You wait and see."

She took a basket of lemons from the larder and sliced each lemon in half. Rose helped her twist them around and around on the lemon squeezer until only the pulpy rind was left. They poured the juice into a pitcher, added water, a scoop of sugar and stirred it vigorously. Rose took a taste from the edge of the spoon.

"Mmmm, a little tart and not too sweet. Just the way I like it."

Aunt Ellen covered the mouth of the pitcher with a net to keep the flies away. The edge of the net was fringed with beads and they tinkled against the pitcher as she set it on a tray.

"There. We'll be ready when they call for it," she said, looking satisfied. "Now Rose, do you mind going into the garden and picking the peas? I'll put a few extra place settings out for dinner. Master Jack's friends will be staying for dinner tonight, I'm sure." She straightened her apron and bustled away down the hall.

The air in the kitchen was hot and claustrophobic. Rose opened the screen door. It was a relief to feel the cool breeze creeping up from the water. She hopped down from the veranda and peeked around the side of the house.

Master Jack and his friends were playing a noisy game of croquet. They'd taken off their suit jackets and rolled up their sleeves for the game. Their suspenders marked a V across each crisp, white shirt back. Rose could see Jack was an accomplished player. He was tall, with a dapper moustache and an easy laugh.

Nearby Mr. O'Reilly was asleep, comfortably sprawled in a lawn chair at the edge of the game. His legs stretched out in front of him, and his beard rested like a fluffy white nest on his shirt front.

On the far side of the garden, Rose could see Miss Kathleen at an easel, intent on her painting. She wore a white gauzy dress with billowing sleeves and a wide-brimmed hat. Just at that moment, she happened to look up from her painting. She spotted Rose and waved. "Rose. Would you like to come over and see what I'm painting?" she called.

Rose edged past Jack's croquet game and the still-sleeping Mr. O'Reilly.

"Oh, Miss Kathleen, it's beautiful, absolutely beautiful!" Rose exclaimed. It was a view of the house and garden. "There's no mistaking the house. I'd know it anywhere. I had no idea you could paint so well."

"How kind of you to say so, Rose. But I'm afraid I am not really much of an artist. It's so difficult to get the light the way it should be. I just dabble really," said Miss Kathleen, modestly. But Rose could see she was pleased.

Miss Kathleen picked up the brush and added a few strokes. "I used to do a lot of painting when I was younger. Not so much now, I'm afraid. This painting is actually something I did years ago. Do you see? We had the tennis net set up then, instead of croquet. Father said he wants it framed and hung in the drawing-room. He doesn't want it tucked away out of sight. But when I pulled it out and looked at it again, I thought it needed a little touching up. There." She added a dab of scarlet. "What do you think?"

"I agree with Mr. O'Reilly. It should be framed."

Miss Kathleen dipped the brush in a cup of greyish water and swirled it around. "Maybe I'll paint something for you one day. A rose perhaps? A rose for a Rose. Would you like that?"

Rose was surprised by the offer. Miss Kathleen paint something for her? She nodded enthusiastically, "Oh yes. Thank you. I'd like that very much. No one has ever painted a picture for me before. And I do like roses, especially yellow ones." She cast her eye about the rose garden. "A soft yellow, like that one," she said, pointing out a rose the colour of soft sunshine, full of hope and happiness, or so it seemed to Rose.

Miss Kathleen smiled. "That is a lovely colour, I agree. A soft yellow rose it shall be then."

Rose looked up to see Aunt Ellen coming toward them. Her awkward limp and black attire made her look like an injured crow. "I beg your pardon, Miss Kathleen," she said. "The seamstress from town is here to do your fittings."

Miss Kathleen glanced down at the watch pinned on the front of her dress. Her neck bent gracefully like a swan, serene and elegant. "Oh. Is it that time already? I didn't realize it was so late."

It was the third day in a row that the seamstress had come to the house. She'd been altering the sleeves and neckline on one of Miss Kathleen's ball gowns. Rose had watched the seamstress cutting and pinning and basting. The dress was a beautiful fabric—white silk with sparkles that caught the light like fairy wings. Rose wanted to reach out her hand and touch it. Imagine how it would feel to wear such a dress!

The seamstress would sit at the sewing machine in the corner of the kitchen. She'd peer down through her eyeglasses, her feet would pump evenly back and forth on the treadle and the machine would made a gentle, purring sound as it sewed.

Aunt Ellen had also taken quite an interest in the seamstress's work. Whenever Aunt Ellen had a free moment, she would watch attentively, ask a few questions and take careful note of any tips that might be passed along. Rose knew she was thinking about the day when she might do the same kind of work.

The ball gown was to be part of Miss Kathleen's travelling wardrobe. Lately there had been much discussion and many preparations for her trip. Rose had heard all about it. In just a few months, Miss Kathleen was planning to board a steamer boat and sail across the Atlantic. She'd tour Ireland and England, visiting family friends and relatives. By the sounds of it, she was expecting dozens of invitations to parties, concerts and weekends in the country.

Now Miss Kathleen put down her paintbrush and stepped back, her head tilted to one side, to study the painting. "Maybe just a touch more scarlet? What do you think, Ellen?"

Aunt Ellen stood behind Miss Kathleen and tilted her head in a similar fashion. It reminded Rose of a lady and her shadow—shorter, darker and one step behind.

"You've done a wonderful job, Miss Kathleen. It's an excellent painting. I wouldn't add a thing," Aunt Ellen said.

Miss Kathleen looked satisfied. "Well, I suppose if the seamstress is waiting...."

"Ellen, just the person!" Master Jack called across the lawn. He had taken off his straw hat and was fanning himself with it. "Be a saviour, will you, and bring us out a pitcher of lemonade. We're dying of thirst out here."

"Certainly, sir," Aunt Ellen said and bobbed a curtsy. She caught Rose's eye and winked as if to say, Didn't I tell you?

Mr. O'Reilly woke with a resounding snort, straightened himself in the chair, then fixed his eyes on Aunt Ellen.

"I could do with some tea, and a bit of cake if there's some."

Aunt Ellen bobbed another curtsy. "Yes, sir. Right away."

"Carry on, boys," he said. "Tremendous game. Been enjoying it."

Miss Kathleen and Aunt Ellen walked back to the house, the young men returned to their game and Rose turned toward the water. It glinted and sparkled in the bright light. She should be making a start on the peas—she'd promised Aunt Ellen—but somehow the water seemed to draw her toward it, like a moth to a flame. Her feet moved down the sloping path. She couldn't help herself. Polka dots of sunlight filtered through the arbutus trees. Shimmering reflections danced across the rocks and under the trees on the bank. Rose picked her way across the stones and driftwood toward the bridge. If she'd lost her locket close to the water's edge, she'd have a better chance of finding it now, at low tide.

The beach was soft and muddy near the water. She'd better be careful with her shoes, she reminded herself. Somehow—and Rose couldn't quite understand it—but somehow her shoes always seemed to be muddied and scuffed. Most mornings, they were so dirty she had to take a brush to them and then shine them up with a cloth. Aunt Ellen would click her tongue and shake her head. "How you get those shoes so dirty is beyond me."

Rose unlaced her shoes, rolled her black stockings off and threw them up onto the stony part of the beach. Then she picked up a long, twisted, sun-bleached stick. She held her gingham skirt up around her knees with one hand, the stick in the other, and stepped carefully. The wet sand squished up between her toes. She placed one foot gingerly into the water. It was a cold shock against her hot flesh. But oh! how wonderful on such a hot day. She waded slowly, trying not to stir up the muddy sand, peering down to the bottom and prodding her stick against anything that caught the light.

Rose was completely absorbed in her task when she heard the *splash...splash...splashing* of oars. She straightened up. A small wooden rowboat came floating into view from beyond the far corner of the boathouse. As it moved closer, she recognized the girl from the fancy carriage and her brother—Cynthia and Francis Abbott. The back of the boat, where Cynthia sat, weighed heavily in the water. Francis sat in the middle, straining at the oars.

"Stop that. You're splashing me! You won't be allowed to row again if you keep that up," Cynthia said.

"I'm doing my best."

"Well hurry up. Honestly, Francis! You're hopeless. I could have rowed over here in half the time. And you're way off course too. Why don't you look where you're going?" Cynthia's nettled, impatient voice carried clearly over the water.

Francis twisted around in his seat and scanned the shoreline. When he saw Rose he lifted a friendly hand in greeting.

"Good afternoon," he called out.

Rose acknowledged him with a wave in return. Maybe she'd been wrong about them. She was just about to reply good afternoon, when Cynthia said, "It's that street urchin from the other day. Don't talk to her."

But Francis ignored his sister. "Hot day," he called again.

Rose shielded her eyes against the sun. Cynthia was certainly snobbish. But the boy might be all right. At least he was trying to make an effort. "Yes it is," she acknowledged.

Francis heaved on the oars, bringing the boat closer to the shore. He took off his hat, and ruffled his hair. "Going fishing?"

Cynthia crossed her arms huffily and looked away.

"No. Just looking for something I lost," Rose hesitated. But what harm could possibly come from telling them? "It's a locket. I think I might have lost it somewhere near here."

"What does it look like?"

"It's silver and oval-shaped. About this big," She held two fingers apart. "I'm not sure exactly where I lost it. It could have come off in the water, or on the beach. Maybe up on the lawn there." She pointed to the big house beside the bridge. "I haven't looked up there."

"That's the Grant's house. They're friends of our family. It fact that's where we're headed right now. I'll look around for your locket up there if you'd like."

Cynthia turned around sharply. "Francis! Don't be a complete fool. You don't know the girl. Look at her! She doesn't even have shoes, for goodness sake. For all you know she could be a lying thief."

Rose stood as tall as she could. "My name is Rose and I'm staying at the O'Reilly's—as their guest. And of course I have shoes. I'm just not wearing them right now." She took a hasty breath and added, "I don't lie and I'm not a thief either."

Cynthia sniffed. "Don't believe a word of it. She must be some kind of servant girl," she said and promptly turned her back.

Francis didn't pay any attention to his sister. "Well, nice to meet you, Rose. I'm Francis," he said. "I'll ask the Grants if they've seen the locket." He put his hat back on and picked up the oars.

"Thank you, Francis. It has flowers painted on

the front and inside, if you open it up, it says Courage."

"Courage? Well if I find it, I'll know where you are. Good luck, Rose, and goodbye." He started pulling on the oars. Dip and splash, dip and splash. The sun glinted on the slick wooden blades. "We're going to be even later now, Francis. Thanks to you. You've wasted half the afternoon talking to that girl. We could have been there by now," Cynthia said sourly. "Can't you row any faster?"

The little boat slowly zig-zagged through the water, under the ruins of the bridge, toward the Grant's wharf. Cynthia's high voice prickled across the water, but each time a little quieter, as the boat moved farther and farther away.

Rose turned her head. As she did, something caught the corner of her eye—a dark shape, half in the shadows. She shaded her eyes against the sun. There, on the bank, in the trees by the foot of the bridge, a figure stood watching her. It appeared to be a woman, dressed in black from head to toe, standing as motionless as a statue.

A rash of goosebumps sprung up across Rose's back. How long had the woman been watching her? At first she thought it was Aunt Ellen. Aunt Ellen, in her black dress. But what would Aunt Ellen be doing at the bridge? Surely she would be back at the O'Reilly house, doing her chores.

It was difficult to see the figure clearly. The dark shape blended into the shadows and trees. Rose blinked her eyes, trying to focus. But all she could see were trees now.

It was gone.

8

THE GHOST AT THE BRIDGE

Rose and Aunt Ellen were up to their elbows in sudsy water. The washerwoman was sick and had not come this week, so they had decided to tackle the growing pile of laundry themselves. They had soaked it with soda crystals overnight. Today was wash day. And tomorrow, after everything had dried, they would do the starching and ironing. Rose tied a red and white kerchief over her hair to keep it out of the way. Up and down she scrubbed, up and down against the hard, ribbed scrubbing board. Then she lifted the clothes, wet and dripping, from the huge galvanized washing tub and plopped them into the rinsing tub. She swirled them around with a stick. Then she squeezed out water, wringing them tightly. Her hands were sore, and her skin burned from the strong soap and hot water. She dropped each piece of laundry into a basket until it was heaped over the top. Then she grasped a handle on one side, and Aunt Ellen took the handle on the other. Together, they hoisted up the basket and staggered into the backyard.

They shook out the sheets and towels, smoothing each one along the line and securing them with clothespins. There were trousers and shirts and table linens. And there were Miss Kathleen's dresses and shirtwaists with fancy trims, which required special care. Rose held a particularly fine dress up to herself and spun around.

"How do I look?"

"Rose! That's Miss Kathleen's dress. What would she say if she saw you?" Aunt Ellen shot her a warning look.

Rose hung it on the line but the next item she picked from the basket was a much beribboned shirtwaist she'd seen Mrs. O'Reilly wear. She couldn't help but hold up the shirtwaist as well. "And how about now, Aunt Ellen? How do I look now?"

Aunt Ellen's mouth began to twitch. "You look all trussed up like a Christmas turkey," she said. Then she clapped a hand over her mouth and began to giggle.

They laughed and laughed until they fell down and the grass tickled their backs. And there they lay, not wanting to get up again, not wanting to go back to work. The wind whipped and snapped the laundry on the line. The clouds floated overhead like ships in full sail. It was easy to ignore the rest of the laundry waiting in the basket.

"There's a ghost at the bridge. Have you heard?" Aunt Ellen said. "Everyone's talking about it."

"What are they saying?"

"They say at night the ghost appears near the bridge. It's dressed all in black and it carries a lantern. It walks back and forth near the water's edge, but if you try to get close to it...," She paused and looked directly at Rose. "It disappears."

"Dressed all in black?" Rose sat straight up. She had seen a mysterious person by the bridge. Someone dressed all in black. Could that have been the ghost? She turned to Aunt Ellen. "You haven't been near the bridge in the last few days, have you?"

"The bridge? Oh no. I haven't been there in ages. Not since the accident. But about this ghost...," Aunt Ellen continued. "The Chinese cook at the Tyrwhitt-Drakes saw it last night at the bridge. He told their parlourmaid and she told me this morning. He said it happened late at night. Pitch black. He saw it floating a few feet above the ground, over near the bridge. It was carrying a red light and gave him such a fright he could barely speak. He watched it float by the Grants' house, and then the Tyrwhitt-Drakes' house and then go up by our house. That's when it disappeared."

Rose felt the blood tingle in her veins. "The ghost came from the bridge up to this house? Why would it come here?" Her voice was barely a whisper.

Aunt Ellen shrugged. "People say it's something to do with the accident at the bridge."

Rose turned this over in her mind. Could it be the spirit of someone who had died at the bridge? Then a sudden thought struck her. Mrs. Scott! Mrs. Scott's spirit. But then maybe it was not a woman at all. Maybe it was a man. Could it be her father's spirit coming to see her again? To make sure she was all right? Why else would a ghost come to the O'Reilly house?

❧

"Yoohoo, Jess!" A sing-song voice called. It was Libby, coming in her direction.

Jess blinked her eyes rapidly as Rose and Aunt Ellen faded away.

Libby stood, looking down at the box of strawberry jam. "I came out to see how you're getting along."

Jess looked down at her hand. She was still holding the label she'd retrieved from the bushes. "Just this last one, and then I'm done," she said as she hurried to join Libby.

Libby regarded her closely. "Are you all right? You look white as a ghost."

"Oh yes. I'm fine," Jess tried to sound nonchalant even though her heart was pounding. The Abbotts! Wasn't that the name of the family who had lived in her own house? Yes. She was sure that was what her mother had said—the Abbotts. So, Cynthia and Francis Abbott had lived in Jess' own house! Even her own bedroom—that sickly pickle-green colour—that could have been Cynthia's bedroom!

Jess licked the label and stuck it on the last jar.

"There. All done," she said, hoping Libby wouldn't notice how her hand was shaking. It felt like hours had passed during her vision. What must Libby think of her taking so long to do a simple task?

"I'm sorry, Libby," Jess apologized. "I've been so slow sticking these on."

A bemused look crossed Libby's face. "Slow? What are you talking about, Jess? I asked you to do it only a few minutes ago."

A few minutes! That entire vision—the rag boy, the croquet game, Francis and Cynthia in the rowboat—had occurred in only a matter of minutes.

"You've been a big help, Jess. Thank you," Libby was saying. "By the way, I meant to tell you, I've heard some very nice comments about you from some of the visitors. They really enjoy hearing what you have to tell them about the house. Sometimes I think you know more about the O'Reillys than I do!"

Jess blushed. What would Libby think if she knew the reason? Jess had actually seen the O'Reilly's, not just read about them in a book.

Libby picked up the box of strawberry jam. "I'll take this back into the gift shop. Could you cut some flowers next? Make sure you get a few sweet peas too, by the front door. They're just starting to bloom now, and they smell absolutely divine. Bring them around to the back and we can do up some arrangements for the tea garden."

"Okay, Libby."

Jess had only begun to pick the flowers when she stopped. On the other side of the fence, near the road, she could see a row of huge trees towering high above the house. It was a shock to realize they were the very trees that had only been saplings, no more than slender slips, when Rose had the rag boy sharpen the kitchen shears. So many years had passed that the tiny saplings had become gnarled old trees. But to Jess it felt as if Rose had only just run out to the road with a tea cloth filled with cookies. Or waded, bare-legged, through the water—looking for her locket.

Jess continued through the garden, selecting roses and foxgloves and sweet peas. They made a mass of colour in her arms. She took in a deep breath. Oh!—such a wonderful, heady scent.

But Rose didn't like to cut flowers, Jess remembered. She liked to leave them growing in the garden. Then Jess remembered something else—Louisa's story about the staff member who had gone out to cut flowers when something mysterious had stopped her. Could that have been Rose? And would the same thing happen to Jess? Would she, too, feel a ghostly hand against her arm, holding her back?

Jess finished up quickly, hoping Rose would not be too upset by the huge armload of flowers. And as she turned to take the flowers in, she stopped once again. It was like looking at Miss Kathleen's painting all over again. Jess must be standing on the very spot Rose had stood when she'd admired Miss Kathleen's painting that summer afternoon so long ago. It was the very painting that now hung in the drawing-room, the same one that had caught Jess' attention the day of the class tour. She stood, gazing at the veranda. Vines swirled like a waterfall around pillars and posts, over the railing to the ground below. And carried afloat were masses of flowers like sprays of frothy bubbles.

Jess gave herself a shake and continued on to the carriage house, a low building near the gift shop that had been converted into a working kitchen. Several of the older staff were inside, busily making up trays of sandwiches and cakes for the tea garden guests.

"What beautiful flowers!" It was Louisa, the girl who had told Jess the ghost stories. She picked up a plate from the counter and offered her a cookie. "They're still warm. They're really for the customers, but I'll let you have one." She winked and put a finger to her lips.

There was something about the way Louisa did that—the finger to her lips—that reminded Jess of something. She took a bite of the cookie, crispy at first and then dissolving on her tongue. And what was that taste? Almonds?

"Good, isn't it?" said Louisa. "Almond shortbread, one of Mrs. O'Reilly's recipes. Exactly like the ones she used to make."

Jess looked at the remains of the cookie she held in her hand, the same kind of cookie Rose had taken from the kitchen and given to the rag boy.

Louisa put the plate down and wiped her hands on a tea cloth. "I'd better get back to work now. We've got customers waiting. Libby left some vases out for you on the table."

Jess popped the rest of the cookie into her mouth and began arranging the flowers, making sure each vase had some sweet peas. She added water, then carried the first two vases carefully, one in each hand, down the path to the tea garden. A few clusters of people sat in white wicker chairs, sipping tea and nibbling sandwiches. Jess placed a vase down in the centre of the first table. The bright flowers looked cheerful against the white of the table.

"Hey! Look! It's Jess."

Jess' heart sank. Rats and double rats! Maxine and Tiffany were sitting on the far side of the tea garden. They had twisted around in their chairs and were staring in her direction. Across from them sat a bored looking woman and a boy with a bristly haircut wearing a striped T-shirt.

I might as well go and get it over with, Jess decided. Her feet felt like lead as she crossed the lawn.

"What *are* you wearing?" Maxine said, looking Jess up and down. She did not speak any quieter, even though Jess was now standing only a few steps away.

"It's a...It's a...costume." Jess stammered. She looked down at the flowers. They were trembling.

"A costume! What do you think this is? Halloween?" Maxine said with a sneer. Tiffany snickered into her napkin.

The woman across the table looked like a movie star with her sunglasses and bright red lipstick. She stifled a yawn. "Maxine, darling," she said, mildly. "It's quite a nice dress really. Why don't you introduce us?"

Maxine rolled her eyes. "Mom, this is Jess. Jess, Mom." Then as an afterthought she added, "And this is my brother, Bradley."

The boy stuffed a whole cucumber tea sandwich into his mouth. "Can you get me some more lemonade?" he said through the mouthful of food.

"Yeah," agreed Maxine with a nasty smirk. "Get me some too."

Jess could feel her face getting hot. "I'll let Louisa know," she replied. "I've just brought you some flowers." She leaned across the table to set the vase down. And then, just as she was reaching forward, something unexpected happened.

A sudden, clattering crash.

Maxine leapt to her feet. "Look what you did!" she shrieked.

The plate of sandwiches had toppled onto Maxine's lap and then splattered to the ground. Clumps of yellow egg oozed down the front of Maxine's white shirt. The grass at her feet was strewn with triangles of brown and white bread, sliced cucumbers and globs of tuna.

Maxine's mother was on her feet too. "Oh! For goodness sake! Your nice new shirt too." She began wiping off Maxine's shirt with a napkin and shot Jess a dirty look.

People from the other tables were staring.

"I'm sorry. It was an accident," Jess said, her eyes stinging like pinpricks and her nose threatening to sniffle.

"Maxine," the bristle-haired boy at the table said. "You're wearing the sandwich I wanted. And I think you should know that yellow is definitely not your colour."

"That's not even funny, Bradley," Maxine retorted with a glare. "Tell him to shut up, Mom."

That's when Libby came bustling over to the table. "Is there a problem here?" she asked.

"It's that Jess person," Maxine's mom announced. "She deliberately dumped sandwiches all over my poor daughter. You should fire her!"

9

BREAKING THE RULES

Jess picked up her skirt and fled up the path to the back veranda. She yanked open the screen door and rushed inside. The scullery was dark after the harsh brightness outdoors.

Everyone would be thinking she'd dumped the sandwiches on purpose. Either that, or they'd think she was a great big klutz. And Libby would probably say she couldn't work here anymore. Who'd want a volunteer who dumped sandwiches all over the guests?

Jess wiped her eyes with the back of her hand and it came away, salty-wet. The tears were starting to roll down her face. She squeezed her eyes shut. It wouldn't do to let anyone see her cry, especially Maxine and Tiffany. But where could she go? The little door to the attic! Of course. No one would think to look for her up there.

She tried the doorknob. Locked. But Jess knew where Libby kept the keys in her office. She peeked in. Good, no one was there. Her eyes darted to the jangle of keys tossed on the desk. She snatched them up, ran back to the door and fumbled impatiently with the lock.

I shouldn't be doing this, she warned herself as the key turned. I don't have permission to go up to the attic. On top of that, I'm already in big trouble. But her feet refused to listen. They flew up the steep, narrow steps as if they had a mind of their own.

It was hot and stuffy in the attic. Jess turned to the left, and there, tucked in under the eaves, was Rose's room.

It was small and plain—the whitewashed walls, the bare wooden floor, the little servant's bell over the door—all the same as when Rose had slept there. The small window still peered out over the roofline and chimney tops—the same bleak view, if you could call it a view. Still, it allowed enough light to brighten the room.

Even though the room itself had not changed, other things had. Cardboard storage boxes now cluttered the space. Much of the furniture had been removed. What little remained was stacked to one side. Two iron bed frames were propped up against the wall. The smaller one was white and the other, black. Jess ran her hand over the peeling white paint of the small headboard. That would have been Rose's bed. And the black one would have been Aunt Ellen's.

Jess sat down on one of the boxes. She pulled a tissue out of her pocket, wiped her eyes, blew her nose, and thought back over the scene in the tea garden. She could remember reaching across the table with the flower vase. And there was something else she remembered, something that troubled her. She recalled seeing her own hand take the edge of the sandwich plate and tip it over. Her own hand! But she had not meant to do that at all. What could have possessed her to do such a thing? And the way her feet had run up the stairs even though she knew she shouldn't. What was happening to her? It felt like she was loosing her grip—that she couldn't control herself anymore. Maybe the part of her brain that relaxed enough to let the visions happen had relaxed a little too much. It was a scary thought.

"Rose?" she whispered aloud. "Are you there?"

She waited. A minute passed and then, despite the stifling heat of the attic, a shivery chill crossed the back of her neck and tingled all the way down her spine like a drop of ice water....

Strains of music wafted into the little attic room, drifting up through the floorboards and floating out the window into the hot night air. Rose lay in bed, listening. The O'Reillys were having a party downstairs. Although it was getting very late Aunt Ellen had not yet come to bed.

"Let's have some dancing!" Rose heard a man's voice say. She recognized it as Jack's.

"Ooooh, let's!" a chorus of ladies' voices replied. The piano started up again, a lovely lilting melody. Rose felt a pang of longing deep in her chest. If only she could be downstairs too, playing the piano as she used to when she'd lived at Mrs. Scott's. It had been such a long time since she'd played.

Perhaps—and her heart beat faster with the thought—she could tiptoe downstairs and have a peek. What harm could it do after all? And if she was careful, no one would see her.

And so, very quietly, and just in her white cotton nightgown and bare feet, she crept down the dark narrow stairs. She cracked the door open at the bottom. No one was in the hall.

Rose huddled into a dark, shadowy corner of the hallway, making herself as small as possible. Directly across the hall, in the dining room, the party was in full bloom with music, laughter and the clinking of glasses. The big dining table had been pushed to one side and the carpet rolled up. Almost out of view, on the far side of the room, Mrs. O'Reilly sat, playing the piano.

Rose pressed back farther into the shadows. The dancers were waltzing around the room, swinging past the doorway view and then out of sight again. If anyone happened to glance out the door at just the right moment, they would surely see her.

Jack was tall and handsome in his black dinner suit. His dancing partner was a beautiful young lady with white rosebuds pinned in her dark hair. Before the song had finished, Jack waltzed by with a new partner. This one was just as beautiful. Jewels glittered at her neck, and she, too, was swept out of sight.

Then Mr. O'Reilly pulled Miss Kathleen to her feet and they danced past the doorway. Her dress was a swirl of sea-green and frothy white lace. It swished like a wave as she whirled around and around.

What would happen if Aunt Ellen came down the hall and into the dining room at this very moment? Would Jack come to her side as she entered? Would he take her by the hand and waltz her around the room?

It could happen, couldn't it? Jack, such a gentleman...and her Aunt Ellen? Wouldn't it be nice if money and social standing didn't matter? Perhaps Jack would look past that, look past the limp and see how pretty and kind and good-natured Aunt Ellen was. Rose could picture the two of them dancing together. And the more she thought about it, the more she hoped it would happen.

The song whirled on and on. Rose peeked around the corner, but the hallway to the kitchen remained empty. All too soon the song had finished, and Aunt Ellen had not appeared.

The dancers clapped and called, "Let's have another one. Another waltz."

The music started up again. Perhaps Aunt Ellen will come now. But Rose did not feel quite as certain as before. What if Jack did not go to Aunt Ellen's side when she appeared in the doorway? What then? Aunt Ellen would shrink quietly into the background, stay out of the way of the dancers and clear away dirty cups and saucers. Rose hated the thought. She couldn't bear to watch it happen. No, she'd rather keep that other picture in her mind, the picture of Jack and Aunt Ellen dancing together.

Rose tiptoed back upstairs and crawled into bed. She lay there, unable to fall asleep. Much later, she heard the guests calling out their cheerful goodnights and the door closing behind them. Then, eventually, Aunt Ellen's slow, tired footsteps trod unevenly up the stairs. The bedsprings protested, creaking as she lay down. There was a deep sigh, and then the house was quiet.

Rose woke the next morning and was surprised to see Aunt Ellen sitting, completely dressed, on the edge of her bed, studying Rose with a serious expression.

"I have something to ask you, Rose. Do you remember anything about last night?"

"Yes...There was the dinner party and the dancing...."

"No. I mean after that. After everyone had gone to bed."

"No. Why?"

"Well, Rose. This may come as a shock but...I think you're the ghost."

"The ghost?" Rose sat straight up. "The ghost by the bridge?"

Aunt Ellen nodded. "I think you are, Rose. I saw you last night...sleepwalking! You were sleepwalking, but at first I didn't realize it. It was so hot after I came to bed, you see. I had trouble falling asleep. Then I heard you get up and go downstairs. You didn't say a word. I thought you'd come right back but you didn't. I waited and waited and then I began to get worried. Finally I went downstairs and looked through the house and outside on the veranda. But you weren't there."

Aunt Ellen took a deep breath. "And then, just when I thought I would have to wake up Mr. O'Reilly and Master Jack to help search for you, I saw through the darkness a light from across the lawn. It was a reddish light, and it came up from the water, swinging back and forth as it moved toward me. I thought it must be the ghost that people have been talking about. I really and truly thought it was the ghost. It scared me half to death.

"But it wasn't the ghost at all. It was you, Rose, carrying the lantern from the scullery, the conductor's lantern—the one with the red and white globe. You came in the back door, just in your nightgown with a dark blanket wrapped around you. Your shoes were all muddy. I said, 'What were you doing out there in the middle of the night? You gave me such a fright.' But you didn't reply. You seemed to be in a daze. You blew out the flame and put the lantern back on the shelf. You took off your shoes and went upstairs to bed. And all without saying a word." Aunt Ellen paused. "Do you remember any of this, Rose? Anything at all?"

As Rose had listened to Aunt Ellen's account, a hazy memory had begun to form, like a wisp of smoke. And as she thought about it, it started to take shape—become more solid. "I remember a dream," she said slowly. "In the dream, I'm searching for my locket, but something is wrong with my eyes. I feel very nearly blind. I have to strain so hard to see, and I don't think I'll ever find it."

"There! You see! That wasn't a dream," said Aunt Ellen. "You really were down by the water last night, searching for your locket. And the reason you were having trouble seeing was because you only had the light from the lantern. It would have been pitch black except for that. I expect that was not the first time either. You must have gone before, on other nights. That would explain why people have been seeing a light down by the water. And why I've been finding your shoes, all caked in mud, by the back door in the mornings."

"So," Rose said. "*I* am the ghost." She hugged her knees to her chest. It was hard to believe she'd gone to the beach night after night to search for her locket— and all without realizing it. "But I've never been sleepwalking before. At least, not that I know of," she added.

Aunt Ellen bit her lower lip. "You know," she said, "I've heard of other people sleepwalking. It seems that it happens when a person is troubled. And you certainly have had troubles of late, Rose—the accident and losing your father and all. But I think this sleepwalking will pass. I really do." She nodded as if she was trying to convince herself.

Outside their attic window, the morning sky was brightening. The sun had climbed above the treetops. Birds were twittering and squabbling outside. Aunt Ellen jumped up with a start. "Goodness! The time! I'd better get downstairs before the day's half over." She paused briefly at the door. "Don't worry. I won't tell anyone what happened last night. Let them go on thinking it's a ghost."

After Aunt Ellen had gone downstairs Rose paced back and forth in her room. Sleepwalking! And people thought *she* was the ghost! How amazing that she could navigate the rocks and logs, in a half sleep, and with only the light from the lantern to see by. And not just once, but many times! It seemed the girl who rose out of her bed at night and went down to the beach was someone else, a stranger. It gave Rose an unsettled feeling, like a swarm of bees under her flesh. But as she considered it, everything began to make sense. Everything that is, except for one thing. If she was the ghost, then who was the lady in black she'd seen by the bridge?

Rose washed and dressed, but she couldn't shake the strange, unsettled feeling—it followed her as closely as a shadow. She knew what she would do if she was at Mrs. Scott's. She would sit down at the piano and play and play, as long as it took to feel better, to feel that some sense of order had restored itself. And as she thought about this, an idea began to form in her mind. Perhaps she could play one of the O'Reillys' pianos. There had to be a time when the house was empty, a time when she could secretly play. She waited impatiently as the hours ticked by, but there always seemed to be someone in the house. Finally the moment came. It was mid-afternoon. The O'Reillys had taken the carriage and gone to visit friends. Sing and Moon were outside pulling up carrots and Aunt Ellen was at the side garden, chatting with the Tyrwhitt-Drakes' parlourmaid from next door.

Rose could hear Aunt Ellen saying, "The O'Reillys have been very kind letting us stay here, but we can't impose on them much longer. I've been out looking at boarding houses, and I'm sure I must have seen every one in town by now. It's criminal what they charge. Anything decent is far beyond my wages. And there's two of us now to think of, what with my Rose. Honestly, I don't know what I'm going to do."

The Tyrwhitt-Drakes' maid had an impish voice. "Now, Ellen! Don't go telling me you have no future prospects. Get yourself a rich husband. That'll solve your problems for you."

Rose suddenly remembered the image she'd had last night, the image of Jack and Aunt Ellen dancing together. She could see them dancing around and around the room, laughing as they went. The thought floated, lovely and dreamlike in her mind.

Rose slipped back into the house. Except for the ticking of the kitchen clock, everything was quiet. She tiptoed to the dining room door and looked across the room to the piano in the corner. But there was another even better piano in the drawing-room. It was further away from the kitchen, in case anyone should come back into the house.

Rose opened the red baize door—exactly what Aunt Ellen had told her not to do—and stepped from the servants' side of the house, into the O'Reillys' side. Then she closed the door quietly behind her.

The drawing-room piano was finely made, the darkest shade of chestnut-brown, and elegantly fitted with candle holders. It was nothing at all like Mrs. Scott's scratched and battered piano.

The carpet felt thick and spongy beneath her feet. She sat down on the piano stool and held her hands over the keys. Then she played one note—a clear tone, perfectly formed, like a crystal. Slowly, slowly, it faded away. Rose closed her eyes and listened until only the memory of the sound was left.

Then, very softly, she played a simple tune. The music came easily, a piece she had learned long ago. It flowed down through her fingers, out from the piano and into the room. The music surrounded her and comforted her. Everything that had troubled her over the past month—the accident at the bridge, the deaths of her father and Mrs. Scott, the problem of where to live—all these things seemed to fade as the music took over.

As soon as she finished the first song, she started another. But she had only just begun when a gruff voice spoke behind her.

"What do you think you're doing?"

Rose snatched her hands off the keys and twisted around. It was the gardener, Mr. Norman. He was standing outside in the garden, looking through the open window. The striped canvas awning shadowed his face, but she could see his hard eyes fixed on hers.

"I...I...," Rose stuttered.

"You're messing with the O'Reillys' things, that's what you're doing. I've got a good mind to tell the Missus. You'd be out on your ear in no time. You and your Aunt Ellen sent packing." One corner of his lip raised in a sneer as he spoke.

Fear gripped the pit of her stomach.

"Please, Mr. Norman. Please don't tell anyone," she pleaded.

"Fancy yourself some sort of fine lady, do you? Loitering 'bout playing pianos. You're no more a lady than that aunt of yours. Cut from the same bolt of cloth. You's a common servant girl if ever I saw one. Peeling potatoes, scrubbing floors. That's your lot."

Rose stood up and started to back away. "I shouldn't have come into the drawing-room. I know that. I'm very sorry."

"Hmmmph," he growled. "And on top of it all, I see you've been neglecting your chores."

"Oh...." Rose snapped her mouth shut as she remembered. The pig! She'd forgotten to feed the pig. She'd been so thrown off her routine that morning—learning about the sleepwalking and waiting for the right time to play the piano—that she'd completely forgotten Daisy.

Mr. Norman turned and stalked away.

How foolish she'd been! And what a mean old man Mr. Norman was. Suppose he did tell the O'Reillys. Would Aunt Ellen lose her job? Rose was ashamed to think of the trouble she'd cause.

But poor Daisy! She'd be starving. Rose flew straight to the kitchen and grabbed an apron from the hook on the back of the door—not Aunt Ellen's best apron, the crisp, spotless white linen one she used when she served the O'Reillys—but the chores apron. The chores apron was for dirty jobs. It was made of rough cotton, stained and threadbare at the edges. Rose slipped it over her head and it sagged gracelessly, almost to the floor. She crossed the ties twice around her waist, knotted it tightly, picked up the pail of kitchen scraps and ran down the path to the pigpen.

When Daisy saw Rose coming with the feed pail she snorted in hungry anticipation and pushed her nose through the fence.

"Oh, Daisy! I'm sorry I forgot you," Rose said.

She leaned over the fence and dumped some of the scraps into the trough. Daisy grunted happily and gobbled huge mouthfuls of the sloppy food. The pungent smell of the pen wafted up and filled Rose's nose.

"You like that, don't you? Do you want some more?"

She picked up the pail and tipped it over the fence again. But just then, at exactly the worst moment, the handle slipped out of her hand. The pail fell, clattering over the fence and landed with a final *splat* in the mire.

Rose sighed loudly in annoyance. What else could possibly go wrong today? She reached over the fence trying to fetch the overturned pail. But even when she stood up on the bottom rung of the fence and stretched her arm out as far as it would go, the pail was still out of reach.

"Well, I'm just going to have to come in there

with you, Daisy," Rose said, and she opened the latch on the gate. She held her hem high up out of the muck and tried to step carefully. Every time she put down her foot, a rim of brown mud squished up around the edge of her shoe. Every time she lifted her foot, there was a moist, sucking sound. From the far side of the pigpen, Daisy eyed her warily. Food dripped out of the sides of her mouth and down off her chin. She looked even bigger, close up. Her body was as thick and sturdy as a packing trunk.

"It's all right, girl. Don't be frightened. It's only me, your old friend Rose."

Rose stooped to pick up the pail and turned to go. And that's when she saw the gate was standing wide open. She'd forgotten to close it behind her.

But Daisy had seen it too. The pig darted past Rose, almost knocking her off her feet. Out through the open gate and across the yard it shot, swift and sure as a cannonball fired from a cannon.

"Daisy! Daisy! Stop!" Rose chased the runaway pig straight through the muckiest, most slippery part of the pen. "Daisy! Come back," she called over and over again.

But Daisy had no intention of returning to the pen. She galloped, squealing with excitement, across the lawn, around the side of the house and past the kitchen garden. Moon and Sing looked up from pulling carrots. Aunt Ellen and the Tyrwhitt-Drakes' parlourmaid stared, and their mouths gaped open like twin rabbit holes.

Mr. Norman turned around, hoe in hand, planted himself in the pig's oncoming path and swung his arms wide. But the pig would not be stopped. It barrelled past with such force, Mr. Norman was knocked backwards onto the ground.

"Sorry," yelled Rose as she ran past him a second later.

Daisy was still running. She was out on the street and thundering down the road, her short pig legs pumping like pistons. Rose was not far behind, panting for breath, the pail thumping against her legs, her long apron catching and grabbing at her ankles.

They raced past the Tyrwhitt-Drakes' house. And in the next moment they dashed into the Grants' yard and down the side of the house.

Straight ahead in the shade of the trees, an afternoon tea party was in progress. The ladies in their hats and dresses the colours of rose petals were grouped as perfectly as flowers in a vase.

As Rose careened toward them, she could see that this was not just an ordinary tea party. It was a birthday party. A beautifully decorated cake stood in the middle of the table, frosted in pink icing with sugar flowers and garlands. And there, sitting in front of the cake, preparing to blow out the candles, was Cynthia Abbott.

"SQEEEEE...." The party guests turned in surprise as the pig squealed its arrival.

Men shouted. Ladies shrieked and scattered out of the way. But Cynthia alone remained motionless. She sat transfixed, staring in horror at the oncoming pig.

Then Daisy crashed headlong into the table. The cake arched high up through the air, turning gracefully, as if to be admired from every angle. All eyes were upon it. The cake seemed to hang, suspended for one perfect moment, before it fell smashing to the ground.

The cake was ruined beyond all hope. It lay in pieces, a spectacular, disastrous mess. And Daisy—who had finally stopped running—was now rooting through its pink and white remains, snorting in delight.

Slowly the party guests turned their attention from the grunting pig and the shattered cake to Rose. Their shocked faces stared at her, expecting an explanation and, most certainly, an apology. For the first time, Rose became aware of her appearance—dusty and out of breath, the ill-fitting chores apron, her shoes mired in muck and the dripping slop pail.

The only sound came from the pig as she slurped and snorted and gobbled the cake. Then someone started laughing, a muffled giggle at first, but rapidly growing into boisterous, unrestrained laughter. It was Francis, Cynthia's brother.

"Rose, how kind of you to join us," he said. "And thank you for bringing the entertainment. Very funny. I can't think when I've had a better time."

"Francis! It is not funny. What an idiotic thing to say!" Cynthia seethed. "That pig has ruined everything—the party, the cake, my dress. Look! There's frosting all over my new dress. And that servant girl...!" She glared at Rose, and her eyes were as hot and furious as burning embers. "I hold that servant girl entirely to blame."

1 O

THE MAKE-BELIEVE PIANO

Rose sat alone on a log, cupping her chin in her hands and staring miserably at the bridge. How she hated the sight—its wide expanse of nothingness in the middle, the twisted metal and the broken timber at either end. Aunt Ellen had told her that work was about to begin on building a brand new bridge and tearing down the old one. Well, that day couldn't come soon enough! She turned away and made herself look instead at the shoreline across the water.

It was almost dinnertime but she was far too upset to think about eating. Daisy had finally been herded back into her pen, and Cynthia's birthday party was ruined. Rose had made a mess of things, there was no doubt.

Rose picked up a stone, feeling its smooth, round weight. It fit in her palm as perfectly and comfortably as if it belonged there. She squeezed her eyes shut. If only her life could go back to being the way it was before the accident at the bridge. Please, oh please. How she wished it could be true.

But when she opened her eyes again, everything was the same—the ugly ruin of the bridge, the wide stretch of water across the Gorge and the old driftwood log she was sitting on.

No Father. No Mrs. Scott. No piano.

She swung her arm, releasing the stone. It arched up in the air and down again, entering the water cleanly with a *plop*. Then it was gone. Rose watched dejectedly as ripples spread, wrinkling the smooth surface of the water.

She picked up another stone. This one had a sharp, jagged edge and she idly scraped it against the log. It made a mark in the sun-whitened wood. Rose regarded the mark—no more than a feeble scratch— with the merest of interest. But then she brightened. In one quick leap she was on her feet. She bent over and scored another line in the wood next to the first. Then another, and another. Soon she had more than a dozen evenly spaced lines, looking very much like keys on a piano.

She dropped to her knees and placed her fingers between the marks. Although her fingers moved silently, she could hear every note in her head. The music closed in around her, enveloping her completely. She rocked back and forth with her eyes closed as she played. The music was all that mattered. On and on she played until, eventually, she became aware of her surroundings again. A breeze was stirring tendrils of hair across her face. Hard stones were pressing into her knees.

Then her scalp bristled. Was somebody watching her? She peered across the beach. There, in the trees near the bridge, hardly more than a shadow, stood the lady in black.

The ghost! Rose caught her breath. How long had she been standing there watching her?

Cautiously, keeping her eyes on the ghost the whole time, Rose stood up. The ghost did not move. It was difficult to see her clearly—she was too far away. But it looked as if she was dressed entirely in black from the hat and veil that covered her face, down to the hem of her dress.

The figure took a step toward Rose.

"Rose! Rose!" A distant voice called from somewhere behind Rose, up near the house. It was so unexpected, it made Rose jump. She turned to see Aunt Ellen waving at the top of the path.

"Coming," Rose called. She looked back, scanning the trees. But now there was no sign of the ghost. She had vanished.

Rose scrambled up the path toward Aunt Ellen and said, "Did you see her? The lady in black. There, in the trees?"

Aunt Ellen shook her head. "A lady in black? No. I didn't see her."

"She was there by the trees." Rose pointed. "She was standing there when you called me."

Aunt Ellen shook her head again. "No. I only saw you. No one else."

"I'm sure it must have been the ghost."

"Now, Rose. We both know who the ghost really is." Aunt Ellen fixed her with a meaningful look.

Rose felt her face colour. She knew she had let Aunt Ellen down. Not only had she been sleepwalking, but she'd deliberately broken the rules of the house, forgotten her chores and let the pig out of the pen. Aunt Ellen must have called her up from the beach to discuss her behaviour. Maybe she would have to explain herself to the O'Reillys. But the thing that worried her most was the thought that Aunt Ellen might lose her job. And all because of her foolish behaviour.

But Aunt Ellen put a hand on her shoulder and gave it a squeeze. "There now, Rose. Don't look so glum. You've had a bad day, that's all. Come along now. Dinner's waiting."

So Aunt Ellen wasn't cross after all! And she didn't seem worried about losing her job either. When Rose sat down at the kitchen table she suddenly realized her appetite had returned. She took a big helping of roast beef, carrots and fresh yellow corn. Every bite was delicious. She had just taken another piece of bread and was wiping up the last of the gravy when she heard the slow, clip-clopping of hooves and the creak of wheels coming down the road. She peered through the window. There was the rag boy's cart stopped on the road in front of the house.

Rose was not surprised. It was becoming such a common occurrence lately that every day about this time she found herself half listening for his arrival. He wouldn't come to the door but just wait for a few minutes at the road. If she wasn't able to go out right away, he would be gone by the time she arrived. Quickly she whisked a few crusts of bread off the table, excused herself and pushed through the screen door.

"Rose," Aunt Ellen called after her. "Don't let the door—" The door banged shut. "—bang."

"Sorry." Rose grimaced. She always forgot when she was in a rush. She ran out to the road just in time to catch the rag boy.

"Much obliged, miss," The rag boy gave her a grateful smile and took a big bite of the bread straight away. Rose had the distinct feeling that these few crusts of bread was all he'd eaten that day. She watched him swallow it down and take another bite. His skin was the colour of dust and ashes—grey and unwashed.

"What do you think you're doing?" A deep voice grumbled from behind them.

They both turned to see Mr. Norman, his face twisted into a scowl.

"You're giving food to that rag boy again. Don't deny it. I know what you're up to." He turned to the rag boy. "You best be shoving off, if you know what's good for you. There'll be no more free handouts around here. Go on. Off with you. I don't want to see you or your old rubbish cart again."

The rag boy wasted no time. He swung up into the cart, gave a furtive tip of his hat in Rose's direction and flicked the reins. The old horse plodded forward, dragging the creaking cart behind.

"Good riddance," said Mr. Norman, with a disapproving snort. Then he turned to Rose. "Don't be fooling yourself, missy. I'm on to you. You've been nothing but trouble since the day you got here. I'm fixing to tell the O'Reillys about your carrying on—messing with their things, letting the pig run amuck, giving away food to that scoundrel. Food that's not yours to give, mind."

"But that bread would have gone to waste anyway. It would have ended up in the pig's slop pail," Rose protested. But even as she said this, she knew there had been days she'd given the rag boy perfectly good food—food that could have been saved. It all depended on what was handy and who happened to be in the kitchen at the time.

But Mr. Norman was not prepared to listen. He had spotted Sing struggling to push a wheelbarrow over the gravel path. "China boy! China boy. Get over here." Mr. Norman gave the order in the same way he might call a dog to his side.

Sing did as he was told, setting the wheelbarrow down and obediently trotting over.

"China boy, have you seen this girl giving food to the rag boy?"

Rose tensed. She knew very well Sing had seen her do it many times.

But Sing shook his head.

Mr. Norman's face clouded. "Come now. This girl has been stealing food from the kitchen. Admit it."

Sing shook his head again. "No, sir."

"What are you? Daft? Why don't you call a thief, a thief?"

Sing slowly lifted his head and looked directly at Mr. Norman. "I see you take food home from garden. That's all I see."

So! Mr. Norman had taken food as well! Sing's daring accusation seemed to hang in the air long after he had spoken. Mr. Norman gaped at Sing and his body trembled with rage. There was a long, uncomfortable silence.

"What I do is my business. Now get back to work," Mr. Norman finally snapped.

Rose caught Sing's eye and silently moved her lips to form the words, Thank you.

There was the hint of a sparkle back in Sing's eye again. He returned to the wheelbarrow, his pigtail swinging defiantly across his back as he walked.

Mr. Norman studied Rose, narrowing his eyes. "Don't go thinking yourself so fine, missy. Putting on airs. You'll end up a servant just like that aunt of yours."

Rose bit her tongue. Maybe she'd surprise him one day. Maybe she'd become a concert pianist. Until that moment, she had barely allowed herself to consider such a daring notion. But yes, it was true. A concert pianist! That was exactly what she wanted to do.

"I'm surprised your aunt puts up with you," Mr.

Norman went on. "If she has any sense in her head, she'll send you off to the orphanage. Then she could set her sights on catching a husband. But she's not going to get a husband with you hanging around her neck like a great millstone, is she? No sensible man would marry her with you part of the bargain, I can tell you that."

Rose was shocked. Could she be packed off to the orphanage? Was she a hindrance to Aunt Ellen's marriage prospects?

"Well, what makes you think my aunt wants to get married anyway? Maybe she's happy just the way things are," Rose retorted. It was all she could think to say.

Her heart was pounding. Waves of anger pulsed through her veins. What right did he have to speak in such a way? But a tickle of doubt had formed in her mind and it was hard to ignore. Maybe what Mr. Norman said was true.

Footsteps on the stairs. Someone was coming up to the attic. Jess made herself focus on the window in front of her. Her heart was hammering in her chest just as Rose's had been a moment ago—No! Over a hundred years ago. It made Jess feel dizzy at the thought.

Louisa appeared in the doorway. "Oh! Jess. I thought you'd already gone home. I was just locking up the house for the night and I found the door open at the bottom of the stairs. You're not supposed to be up here, are you?"

Before Jess could reply, Louisa took a closer look at Jess. "Are you all right? You look a little shaken up."

"Maybe a little," Jess admitted. She could still feel the remnants of Rose's anger.

Louisa sat down next to her on the box.

"I know. I saw what happened down in the tea garden. It wasn't your fault."

Of course! How could she forget what had happened in the tea garden? It all came back to her in a rush—the horrible look on Maxine's face as the sandwich plate spilled, and the way her mother had said Jess should be fired.

"Do you think Libby will be mad at me?"

"I doubt it. It was only an accident after all."

But Jess wasn't convinced. "It was such a stupid thing to do...."

"Well, it could have been a lot worse. It could have been hot tea. Try not to worry about it." Louisa gave Jess' arm an encouraging squeeze. "Come on. We'd better get downstairs."

Jess locked the door at the bottom of the stairs and returned the key to the office. Please don't let me see Maxine and Tiffany again, she prayed silently to herself as she followed Louisa outside. She peeked down to the tea garden and gave a sigh of relief. Maxine's table was now empty. The plate and the sandwiches had been picked up from the ground. There was no sign that the accident had ever happened.

Then she spotted Libby walking up the path. She was balancing a tray laden with a teapot and clinking cups and saucers. Jess shifted her feet uncomfortably as Libby came closer. It was the moment she'd been dreading, the moment when Libby would tell her she was too clumsy to be a volunteer anymore.

But Libby just smiled and winked. "Good aim," she said as she passed.

The weight of Jess' worries vanished with those two words. She wasn't going to be fired after all.

"See?" Louisa nudged her in the ribs. "She was probably glad you did it. I know I was. That girl deserved it."

There were only two customers left, a pair of elderly ladies with curly white hair. They were gathering up their things and preparing to go as Louisa and Jess arrived to clear away their dishes.

"We've had such a lovely afternoon here," one of the ladies said. "Can you tell us what time we catch the ferry back downtown?"

"There should be one coming in about ten minutes," said Louisa. "Do you mind taking them down to the wharf, Jess? You can show them the rose garden and where the O'Reillys' boathouse used to be. Libby says you're getting to be an expert about this place." Louisa gave her a pat on the back, and Jess felt a warm glow of pride. "I'll just clear away their dishes and then we'll be done for the day."

Jess led the visitors through the garden, describing how Miss Kathleen had selected the different varieties of roses. The ladies listened with interest and Jess was happy to answer their questions. She took them down to the wharf, chatted with them until the little ferry pulled in and waved goodbye as they left.

Just think, she told herself—not so long ago I never could have imagined talking to a couple of strangers. But now I do it everyday, almost without giving it a second thought.

As she climbed back up the ramp, she noticed something on the beach glint brightly in the sun. She stopped and leaned over the railing. Could it be the locket? She scrambled down onto the rocks, taking care that her dress didn't get wet or dirty. But there was no locket there. The object that had shone so brightly in the sun was only a shard of glass.

Jess thought back to the night when she had seen the light under the bridge. Rose! It was Rose holding the lantern. Her ghost still searching for the locket after all these years. If Rose was still searching, that could only mean one thing. The locket was still lost. But what could have happened to it? Maybe someone else found it. Who knows how many people had walked along the beach in a hundred years.

But what if it was still here, fallen into some secret spot where no one had thought to look? Jess studied the stretch of beach that led to the footings of the bridge. It was only a short distance, but the tide was high, and the bank was steep and covered in thick brambles. It was difficult to make it all the way along but Jess was determined. She peered under the prickly vines and down cracks between rocks and pushed aside driftwood to see what was underneath. There were tin cans, an old bicycle chain and shiny food wrappers. But although she searched the entire beach backwards and forwards, there was no sign of the locket.

11

THE DIARY

Jess surveyed her room gloomily. If anything it looked worse than before. Her dad had moved her bed and dresser to the maroon side of the plastic sheet and had started work on the green side. Now the old rotting wainscotting had been torn off from the bottom half of the wall. The bare studs were exposed, all dusty and matted with cobwebs. She could see her dad had also begun stripping some of the wallpaper.

She walked across the floorboards, thick with grit, before she realized the carpet was gone as well. She poked her head out the window and looked down below. There was her dad, throwing an armful of rolled-up old carpeting onto a huge pile of rubbish. "Dad! Hi!" she called down.

He looked up and waved. "Oh, hi there. You're home. I got a lot done in your room today. What do you think?"

"Great." A tickle started in her nose and she sneezed. Dust. Dust. Everywhere dust. That was what she was really thinking.

"Look at all this junk!" he said. He was wearing his old paint-stained work overalls and his hair was thick and white with dust. "I'm going to get the rubbish people to take it away. I would have liked to save the wainscotting, but it was too far gone. And when I started pulling it down, you should have seen all the old newspapers stuck in behind it. That was how they used to insulate these old houses, you know."

"Newspapers?" Jess leaned farther out the window.

"Oh, yeah. Tons of them. An old book, too."

"What kind of a book?"

"Just a small book. Brown. Thin. It looked like some kind of a diary with writing in it. I put it aside for you and your mom to look at. I know how interested you both are in all that history stuff."

Prickles of excitement shot down Jess' arms and legs. A diary! Could it be Cynthia's diary? "Where did you put it?"

"Uhh...let me think. It was stuck down in a crack behind the wood and I pulled it out...and then I wanted to put it in my pocket but it didn't fit...and then what did I do?" He rubbed a hand over his hair and a pouf of dust rose up. "Oh, I know. I put it over in the corner by the window."

Jess checked the floor in the corner by the window. There was no book. She looked all around the room and out in the hall.

Then she leaned over the windowsill again. "Dad. The book isn't here. Did you move it again after that?"

"I don't think so," he called back up. "I thought that's where I put it, in the corner by the window. Maybe it got thrown out with some of the rubbish." He threw a board onto the huge pile of garbage and shrugged his shoulders. "It was just an old book anyway."

Jess raced down the stairs, out the back door and across the grass to the rubbish pile. Her dad took off his gloves and tossed them in her direction. "Better put these on if you're going to go through this stuff. There's all sorts of splinters and nails in there." He wandered back into the house, mumbling something about a cold drink.

Jess put on the gloves and pulled off a layer of boards and the musty old carpeting. Underneath she found more boards, ripped sections of wallpaper and white crumbling chunks of something that looked like plaster of Paris. Then she uncovered some newspapers. They were yellow like brittle parchment and stuck together in a thick mass. She peered at the date at the top of the page, all faded now. *Daily British Colonist*, April 5, 1878. Jess did the calculation in her head. Eighteen years before the accident at the bridge. The columns were small and full of advertisements—"Frederick Reynolds. Butcher, Meats and Vegetables. Purveyor by appointment to Her Majesty's Royal Navy," and "Lamps! Patented founts and holders for gas fixtures."

Then there it was, under the newspapers. A small, worn brown book. Stiff, crackling pages with something musty about its odour. Jess checked the inside cover, holding it away from her shadow and into the sunlight so she could make out the faint, spidery writing. "Cynthia Abbott, her diary, 1896." Jess gasped at the sight. Then she clutched it to her chest, ran back inside, up to her room again and threw herself down on the bed.

The edge of each page was stained yellow as if, long ago, it had been left out in the rain. Several of the pages were stuck together and looked as if they would have to be eased apart gently so they wouldn't tear. Jess stared at the date on the cover: 1896, the very year Rose had lived at the O'Reillys'! She searched through the pages until she came to the day of the accident at the bridge.

MAY 26, 1896

A very disappointing day! Everything went wrong. Father had promised to take me to the military parade at Macaulay Point, but just as we were about to leave, we heard the bad news. The festivities had been cancelled—and simply because the bridge had collapsed and a streetcar had fallen into the water. It makes me cross just to think of it.

Father left me at home and went straight to the

bridge to see if he could help. I was terribly let down and, quite honestly, I can't think when I've spent such a tedious afternoon. He didn't return at suppertime or for hours later. Mother said I mustn't wait up for him and must go to bed at my usual time.

I suspect Francis is meddling with my things and reading my diary.

FRANCIS, THIS DIARY IS ABSOLUTELY PRIVATE. IT IS NO CONCERN OF YOURS AND YOU WILL BE VERY SORRY INDEED IF I EVER CATCH YOU READING IT!!!!

MAY 28, 1896

Father took me to the shops after school today and let me have my choice of anything I wanted. He said I deserved a treat because of my Victoria Day Parade disappointment. I chose a hat with green ribbons and lovely silk flowers. It matches my green velvet dress perfectly. I do believe that soft shade of green is an excellent colour for me. It brings out the green in my eyes yet does not detract from my other features.

Francis insisted on tagging along although it was to be my afternoon with Father. I did my best to ignore him. But after we had picked out my hat, Father said Francis could choose a present as well. (I found this most vexing. I do not think Francis should be indulged in such a way, as it will only spoil his character.) He dillied and dallied until I thought I would scream. Finally, he chose a bag of jelly mints, but he kept them entirely to himself instead of offering to share them.

MAY 29, 1896

The accident at the bridge. The accident at the bridge. For the past three days, that is all anyone ever talks about. I am sick of hearing about it. To my mind it is as dull a subject as long division.

JUNE 1, 1896

I wore my new hat to church yesterday. I could not help but notice a young man across the aisle stealing glances in my direction during the final hymn. I think he must be newly arrived in Victoria as I do not recall seeing him before. I guess him to be sixteen or seventeen and quite agreeable to look at. He was very smartly dressed and Francis would do well to take note.

Francis takes no pride in his appearance. His shirt-tail was not tucked in properly and he refused to set it right—even when I pointed it out to him.

Today we had to take physical education in the school field. Our teacher, Miss Peters, said it would do us good to exercise our lungs in the fresh air. I did my best to keep a positive attitude, but it was no use. I find it perfectly ridiculous to do stretching exercises in public. Anyone may have been passing at the time and seen us. I told Mother and she agrees. She promised she would speak to Miss Peters about the matter.

JUNE 4, 1896

Mother spoke to the teacher today, but the meeting was a dismal failure. I wish I had never asked Mother to get involved. Miss Peters reported that I had failed to apply myself not only in physical education, but also in Canadian history. She told Mother my essay on Confederation was due two days ago and she has yet to receive it. It surprises me that Miss Peters would bring the matter up. Of course I intend to complete the essay, only I have been very busy with other matters of late.

As a result of their meeting, Mother says I must try harder in physical education and I must not complain. As well, and this is the worst of it, she says I must stay in my room until I have completed that silly Canadian history essay. I do not see how that is possible as I have not even started it!

I would much rather go to the fancy dress ball tonight at Regent's Park. I think it very unfair of Mother to insist that I stay at home tonight and I told her so. But all she had to say was that I should have thought of that earlier. I am hardly in the mood to do school work and, quite honestly, I couldn't care less about Confederation. I don't see the point in wasting my time on something that happened before I was born.

Mother is planning to wear her violet silk gown and her diamond bracelet tonight. The bracelet is by far her best piece. I once tried it on myself and I think it suits my arm very well. If the truth be told, I think it looks much better on my arm than on Mother's.

JUNE 7, 1896

After church today, the smartly dressed young man from the pew across, made a point of speaking to Francis. I suspect he wishes to strike up a friendship with Francis in order to gain an acquaintance with me. He is certainly much older than Francis after all, and I cannot imagine they would have many common interests. I made Francis tell me everything about their conversation. His name is Gerald and he is staying with the Grants on Pleasant Street, across the Gorge from us. I have always liked the name Gerald. It has a certain dignity about it. Gerald's family is from New Westminster and his sister has taken ill with the scarlet fever. Apparently the Grants are old family friends and he has come to stay with them for a while so he does not fall ill as well. I asked Francis if Gerald had inquired about me at all. Francis said not, but he probably would not tell me if Gerald had.

Gerald invited Francis to come to the Grants' for a visit next weekend. I am certain the invitation must extend to me as well. I have no doubt that was Gerald's intention. I plan to wear my new hat with the green ribbons.

JUNE 10, 1896
Today my piano teacher suggested I practise every day for the recital. I told her I was far too busy with other things—my Canadian history essay for one. Besides, practising the piano is extremely tedious. She is such a silly woman, always sniffing as if she has a cold.

JUNE 13, 1896
Mother gave us permission to take the carriage, but only if the gardener would drive us. We had him take us to the Grants' to see Gerald. Of course, it was the long way around because the bridge remains impassable. I can't see why the city is taking so long

to do something about that bridge. It is a great inconvenience to us.

Gerald said he was pleasantly surprised to see me. He does have fine manners and I cannot think when I have met anyone as charming. Francis, on the other hand, was terribly selfish and demanded Gerald's attention entirely for himself. They both went down to the wharf to look at Captain Grant's sealing boats and they didn't come back until it was time to go. I had tea with Mrs. Grant and she asked us to visit them more often.

We'd promised Mother to deliver a dinner invitation to the Eberts on the way home. I hope she appreciates the trouble it put us to. Not only did it lengthen our journey considerably, but the weather had become windy and miserable by that point in the afternoon. Just as we were setting off, we came upon the rag boy talking to some sort of riff-raff girl at the side of the road. His cart blocked the road entirely, but they just continued talking as if we had all the time in the world to wait. Finally I had no choice but to speak to them. They are certainly a low sort, inconsiderate and ill-bred. And I have serious doubts about the soundness of the boy's mind—he is so dull and slow. He did finally move the cart to the side of the road, but only with a sullen nature and without offering an apology.

If it wasn't for my sweet and charitable disposition, I would have given them a good piece of my mind.

JUNE 14, 1896
Francis suspects me of having affections for Gerald. I

am certain Francis has been reading my diary, otherwise how would he know such a thing? I have decided to hide my diary where he will not find it, and I have discovered just such a place. It is very cunning, and I am very pleased with myself. He will never think to look for it there.

People are always fussing over Francis and saying what a fine young man he is. If only they knew what I have to endure!

And why does no one say favourable things of me?

JUNE 15, 1896
Finished my Canadian history essay and am feeling very pleased with myself indeed!

JUNE 16, 1896
Mother and Father had their dinner party tonight with the Eberts and the Pembertons. The food was very good—asparagus soup, lamb cutlets with mint sauce, and strawberry cream—but I cannot say the same for the conversation. It amazes me how dull people become when they get older. In the entire evening I can only think of one topic of any interest. It was when Mr. Ebert told us about the ghost at the bridge. He said there have been several sightings of a woman in black carrying a light and floating above the ground. It made goosebumps run up and down my spine to hear it. I'm sure I shall not sleep a wink tonight just thinking about it.

Now that I am getting older, Mother allowed me to stay up a little later. I made a point of reminding Mother when it was Francis' bedtime. He had to go off at the usual time, which is only right since he is still a child.

Besides, it serves him right for reading my diary.

JUNE 18, 1896

The piano recital did not go well at all. The teacher had me play a childish nursery rhyme but the other students were allowed to play much prettier pieces. She said I could use my book since I had not memorized it. Then, when I was partway through, I could hear her sniffing and sniffing directly behind me. It so distracted me, I lost my place and had to begin again.

I told Father I am not taking piano lessons again unless he engages a better teacher.

JUNE 20, 1896

We were expected to be at the Grants' by two o'clock this afternoon for croquet, but we did not arrive until nearly half-past the hour. Mother had the carriage, so all that was left to us was the rowboat.

I am certain Francis was deliberately dawdling just to annoy me. Then, to make matters worse, he wasted time by speaking to that riff-raff girl. I recognized her from the other day when the rag boy's cart blocked our way. She says she is staying at the O'Reillys'—some sort of servant girl I imagine. Her clothes are plain as a pin. I have no time for people like that, but Francis chatted on and on as if they were the best of friends. I could have kicked him.

When we finally did arrive at the Grants' dock and I was getting out of the boat, a most unfortunate thing occurred. My foot slipped into the water and my shoe got wet through. Every time I stepped on it, it made a rude noise. Then, to make matters worse, Francis found it terribly funny and insisted on repeating the sound over and over again. He imitated the sound with his mouth in a way only boys seem able to do—certainly a doubtful talent. But the worst of it was, and it still makes me blush to think of it, he did this in front of Gerald. I was mortified. I cannot think when I have suffered such an indignity.

Of course, I could not play croquet because of my shoe and so I sat and watched the others while it dried. Gerald was a gentleman throughout, quite unlike Francis. He asked if he could move my chair into the shade so I would not become overly heated.

I told Mrs. Grant I am to turn fifteen in a few weeks time and she said I must come for a birthday tea.

JUNE 25, 1896

The last day of school! I gave Miss Peters a china cup and saucer that I bought with my own money. At first, I thought I would buy the prettiest cup and saucer in the store, the one with a hummingbird and a honeysuckle. But I only had twenty-five cents left after getting some lovely white kid gloves for myself. My old gloves had become worn and soiled, and, besides, I have had them almost a year. I am very pleased with my new gloves however. They are neat in fit and look very well on my hand.

So, instead of buying Miss Peters the hummingbird and honeysuckle cup and saucer, I bought the next best set. It was painted with violets and I thought it was still very fine.

Then today at the class party, Miss Peters opened Sue Ann Bolt's gift first, and I could not believe what I saw. It was the cup and saucer with the hummingbird and honeysuckle—the very one I would have bought if I'd had enough money.

Sue Ann Bolt thinks herself far superior to everyone else. I am sure she does not have a grain of modesty in her. She is so selfish and unkind. I am surprised she has any friends at all. But perhaps it is people like me, with sensitive natures, that find it hardest to bear. Mother is always telling me that I must learn to suffer graciously. And I do try. Honestly I do.

We brought our report cards home today and I have passed to the next grade. Miss Peters wrote that my Canadian history essay on Confederation was adequate and I would have received a much better mark had it been in on time. Mother and Father had little to say of this, however.

But with Francis' report, they were quite the opposite. There was nothing but praise for Francis. Father read out all the teacher's comments at dinner. "Francis is an asset to the class." "Francis has an excellent grasp of the multiplication tables."

I had to bite my tongue to stop from adding my own comments.

JULY 11, 1896
I loathe pigs! And I loathe that silly, stupid servant girl. I knew she was riff-raff from the moment I saw

her. It was the most disastrous birthday ever! My birthday cake was ruined and my new dress is covered in frosting—the very first time I wore it, too! I was not even able to blow out my candles. I felt like kicking that girl. Fortunately for her, I am too much of a lady to do so.

Then, to top it all, Gerald informed me that he was going pony riding with Sue Ann Bolt tomorrow afternoon. I cannot describe how much this annoyed me. It is just like Sue Ann to interfere when it should be obvious to her that Gerald favours my company.

I did receive several birthday presents, and some of them were very nice in fact. First thing this morning, Mother and Father gave me the birthday dress. It is white organdie with a fine yellow-flowered print. The sleeves are very fashionable and wide and there is a yellow ribbon sash at the waist. But now, I am afraid it may be spoiled. The birthday cake frosting will most certainly leave a stain.

Mother and Father also gave me a Chinese jewellery box. It is not an ordinary jewellery box. Father says it is the only one of its kind in the world. He designed it himself and had a craftsman make it up for him in Chinatown. The outside is black lacquered with painted trees and birds of all colours. Inside was a little card and this is what was written on it:

"One, two, three, four,
A little treasure in every drawer.
But you must find the secret key
To unlock the jewel box mystery."

Father showed me how it works. Fortunately, Francis was not present at the time.

JULY 12, 1896
Sue Ann Bolt sat next to Gerald at church this morning. The way she throws herself at him is shameful. But the worst of it was that he did not seem to mind her attentions. This was the afternoon they were to go riding together as well. Throughout the entire service I could think of nothing else. It made me so cross I would not speak to them after the service.

Gerald told Francis he will be leaving the Grants' in a few weeks and returning to New Westminster. His departure does not bother me in the least, however. He is not the gentleman I first thought him to be, and I wouldn't care if I never saw him again.

JULY 16, 1896
Mavis handed in her resignation first thing and Mother was in a terrible state. She kept saying, "Mavis shows no consideration," and "Where does that leave us?"

I tried to tell her that the next maid we get will surely be better than Mavis. Almost anyone would be an improvement (which is absolutely true; Mavis is next to useless). But nothing I said would cheer Mother. She just buried her face in a handkerchief and refused to get out of bed.

Naturally, I was out of sorts all morning.

JULY 27, 1896
At dinner today Father made a wonderful announcement. This coming Saturday he has arranged

that we will take the train to Shawnigan Lake for a holiday. We will be staying at the resort for an entire week and our rooms will overlook the lake. I am very excited by the news. Everyone is in good spirits, even Mother. I plan to take my best dresses as surely there will be dances.

JULY 29, 1896
There are only three days until we leave! I have started packing and already I have four cases full. I can't decide if I should take my navy linen skirt with the braid trim or my green skirt with the taffeta lining. Perhaps both.

This morning Francis wanted to go to the Grants' to say goodbye to Gerald. I went along as it was such a fine day, and I had not paid them a visit since my birthday tea. (It still irks me to think of it.) As usual, Francis dragged Gerald away the first chance he got, without a thought to anyone else. They were down at the construction site of the new bridge for more than an hour and when they returned what do you think Francis had found? The very locket the O'Reillys' servant girl had lost. It is exactly the way she described it, silver and oval-shaped with painted flowers on the front. When I opened it and read the inscription, I knew for certain that it was the one.

The locket is beautifully made. I can't help but wonder how a servant girl would come into possession of such a fine piece. I am not one to make false accusations, but I hardly think she could have come by it honestly. It is a terrible thing to think that one's possessions may be subject to thievery by one's own servants!

The one unfortunate thing about the locket is that the chain has been broken. Francis says that it must have been wrenched apart and that is how she lost it. Francis was so eager to return the locket to the servant girl, I hardly had time to speak two words to Gerald. But when we were leaving, Gerald took my hand to help me up to the carriage and I am certain he held it a little longer than necessary. It made me think that perhaps Gerald does fancy me after all. I decided it was only fair to give Gerald a second chance and I told him he had my permission to write to me.

But although I have a generous heart and have forgiven Gerald, I can never forgive that O'Reilly servant girl. The way she ruined my birthday was inexcusable. And because of that, I do not regret what I did next. When we were driving over to the O'Reillys', I took the locket from Francis' pocket. It serves the girl right. Besides, Mother is always saying, "He who is careless with his belongings does not deserve to have them."

Francis doesn't know of this, of course. He never will. I have decided to hide it in my Chinese jewellery box. It will be a perfect place and I know it will remain a secret there.

Jess skimmed the rest of the diary quickly. Sometimes many weeks would pass without an entry. Other times Cynthia would write a lengthy note, usually complaining about one thing or another and often about Francis. But even though Jess checked every page, there was not another mention of Rose.

Jess closed the book. Her muscles felt so twitchy with excitement she jumped up and paced back and forth from the window to the door. Her head was swimming with everything she'd learned from the diary.

The next day at Point Ellice House, Jess tiptoed back up the stairs to Rose's room. She couldn't help herself. Here she was, again, going upstairs without permission. But still, her feet stepped quietly up one stair after another until she reached the top.

Her face felt flushed with the heat. She could feel perspiration on her forehead and the nape of her neck. The blue dress hung heavily against her skin. She pushed and pried at the window, and finally she was able to open it a crack. In came a whiff of fresh air, a welcome relief. She closed her eyes. Just relax, she told herself. If nothing happens, then nothing happens.

Everything was quiet. The only sound was the faint *tick tick* of her watch. Then, just as she was about to give up, a soft, cooling breeze shifted the air around her. The back of her neck prickled.

It was a familiar feeling now.

"Aunt Ellen," Rose said. "I'm sorry for all the trouble I've caused you. Ever since I've come here, there's been one problem after another. You have to find another place to stay because of me. There was that time with the pig and sleepwalking too. I think what Mr. Norman says is true. You'd be better off without me."

"Well, for heaven's sake, Rose! Don't go listening to him," Aunt Ellen replied. She'd been beating a rug outside in the yard, but had stopped to wipe her brow. "And what a foolish thing for him to say. He's got it all wrong. There's nothing that makes me happier than the two of us being together."

"But he says you'd be able to get a husband if it wasn't for me."

"Well! The nerve of that man! He should mind his own business. You know, Rose, I'll tell you something, but you must promise never to speak a word of this to another soul."

Rose leaned forward.

"Mr. Norman asked to court me some time ago but I turned him down. He's too old and too mean-tempered for me. I'd much rather grow to be an old spinster than get involved with the likes of him. I expect his nose is out of joint because I refused him. That's what's bothering him and that's why he's talking such nonsense."

"So you're not thinking of sending me to the orphanage?" Rose asked.

"Of course not! Is that what you've been thinking?" Aunt Ellen looked shocked. "All that concerns me is that we remain together."

But there was still a doubt in Rose's mind that wouldn't rest. "But what if you want to get married? Wouldn't it be easier if you didn't have me?"

"We're together now and that's the way it will

stay, whether I marry or not. Besides, I'm not looking for a husband. I'm not one of those foolish girls who throws herself at the first man to tip his hat."

"What about Jack?"

"Jack? Master Jack O'Reilly?" Aunt Ellen laughed out loud. "What a notion! I'm no fancy society lady. And to be honest, Rose, I've never taken the trouble to look at him twice. He's just one of the O'Reillys to me."

Rose swallowed hard. Ever since the night she'd crept downstairs to watch the dancers, she'd kept the imaginary picture of Jack and Aunt Ellen tucked away in her mind. She could see them dancing together, swirling around and around. But now, with Aunt Ellen's words, the dancers froze and their images began to fade from her mind, slipping away like melting snow.

"Well, I'd better finish this rug off." Aunt Ellen picked up the rug beater again. Its wide wicker loops fanned out in a graceful filigree. Even though it looked delicate as lacework it proved itself surprisingly sturdy for the job. *Whack. Whack. Whack.* With each blow, a new cloud of dust rose, fog-like, into the warm summer air.

Rose moved away from the dust. She crossed the lawn and followed the path through the trees down to the beach. She walked slowly along the water's edge, scanning the pebbles, driftwood and seaweed as she went. If only she could find her locket. Then, surely, the sleepwalking would stop and there would be one less thing to worry about.

She found herself at the log she had scratched

with the rock to look like piano keys. She knelt down, her knees pressing into the hard stones, her hands posed over the makeshift keys. Her eyes closed. The music formed itself in her mind. It filled her head like a rich, thick liquid pouring into a jar.

When she looked up at last, there—directly in front of her—was the lady in black. Rose gasped and jerked her hands back from the keys.

The lady was near the trees where she had stood before. She was half hidden in the shadows, her clothing jet-black from head to foot.

"Who are you?" said Rose. Her voice was unsteady. "Are you a ghost?"

The lady did not speak. She took a step toward Rose and then another. Her arm raised, the hand trembling.

Rose jumped to her feet and stepped backwards. "What do you want with me?" she said.

"Please...." the lady replied. Her voice was barely a sigh.

And then the mysterious lady appeared to shrivel and wither, just as a leaf does when it is caught in a flame. She crumbled to the ground like ashes. And there she lay, deadly still.

12

MRS. CAMERON

Rose crouched beside the woman's crumpled body. She touched the dress gingerly, with just one fingertip, almost expecting the figure to vanish in front of her. But the fabric had substance. It was real. The woman was not a ghost after all. Rose laid her hand on the woman's shoulder. The thin bones underneath the fabric felt fragile, like a sparrow's. She shook the woman's shoulder gently.

"Ma'am? ma'am!" she called.

But the woman did not respond. Rose was not even sure she was breathing. A veil—thin and fine like a spiderweb—covered the woman's face. Rose lifted the veil away. She was an old woman. Her skin was pale, almost colourless, and it was crossed with wrinkles. It looked like a piece of paper that had been crumpled into a tight ball and then smoothed out again.

Rose bent closer. And then—yes! she could feel it—a faint, warm breath against her cheek. The woman was still alive.

Rose shook the thin shoulder again, more vigorously this time. "Wake up. Wake up. Please open your eyes."

But, still, the woman did not stir. She lay limply on the rocks like a tangle of seaweed tossed up on the beach.

Rose's mind was racing. She would have to get help. She would run up to the house and call for a doctor. But just as Rose leapt to her feet, the old woman's eyes flickered open. Immediately, a look of alarm crossed her face.

Rose dropped to her knees again. "Don't be afraid," she said gently. "I think you fainted. But you'll be all right now."

The old woman stirred herself, straightened her folded limbs and tried to sit up. She was so frail, Rose needed to support her across the shoulder blades to steady her.

"I'm sorry...I'm sorry to have troubled you." The woman seemed flustered.

Rose studied her with concern. "You're so weak. Are you ill? Have you eaten today?"

The old woman shook her head. There were tears in her eyes.

"Well," Rose said thoughtfully. "I would like to help...."

But how? She couldn't take any more food from the O'Reillys and risk being caught by Mr. Norman again. Then she pushed her fingers into her pocket and pulled out a coin. It was all she had, another penny Aunt Ellen had insisted she take. "Here. Please take this," Rose said. "I know it's not much but you can buy yourself something to eat."

The old woman looked bewildered but she did not take the money. Instead, she looked into Rose's face. "Dear girl." Her eyes were still moist. "You would do that for me...a stranger?"

Rose nodded. "I want you to have it."

The old woman pulled a folded handkerchief from her sleeve and dabbed her eyes. "But don't you need it yourself?"

"I have everything I need. I am not hungry, but I can see that you are. Please take it."

The old woman smiled sadly. She fidgeted with her handkerchief, then finally looked at Rose. "What a generous girl you are. But I can't take your money. For me, it's not a question of money you see...."

But Rose was no longer listening. She had spotted a workman setting up his surveying equipment near the bridge. "I'll be right back," she called over her shoulder as she ran across the beach.

"Excuse me!" she said when she reached the man.

"Do you have any food with you? Anything at all?"

The man just looked at her, clearly surprised by her request.

"I can pay you." She pulled out the coin. "Here. It's all I have. Please. I would be very grateful."

The man hesitated, then picked up his canvas satchel. "I have a few things for my lunch." He pulled out an apple and some cheese. "Will this do?"

"Oh, thank you!" Rose hastily thrust the money into his hand, snatched up the food and ran back to the woman.

"How I can thank you?" the woman said after she'd nibbled a few bites.

"There's no need," Rose assured her. "Are you thirsty? Maybe I can get something for you to drink."

The woman shook her head. "No, my dear. This is more than enough."

"Tell me, why do you come here?" asked Rose. "I've seen you here before."

The old woman sat up straighter. "Not so long ago, at this very spot, I suffered a terrible loss." Her voice was quiet, barely a whisper.

"What happened?"

"My dear daughter Allison was on the streetcar that went down when the bridge collapsed. She was...," she paused. "My dear Allison did not survive," she added finally.

The woman wiped her eyes. "I blame myself. I never should have let her take the streetcar that day. When she left, she kissed me and said she'd be back by dinnertime. If only I'd known. I could have stopped her then. You see...Allison was all I had."

"How did you find out what happened?"

"Dinnertime came and went and she still had not come home. Then there was a knock at the door. It was a policeman. As soon as I saw him, I knew something was wrong. He told me about the accident." She took a long, shivering breath. "And ever since, I've felt nothing but grief and misery in my heart. I cannot sleep. I cannot eat. I do not want to see my friends. Sometimes, I stay in bed all day. The only time I leave the house is when I come here, to visit the bridge."

She looked toward the bridge. "I like to pray here, where her soul is," she said in a voice, even quieter than before.

Rose did not speak for a moment. She had to swallow hard to ease the tight knot that had formed in her throat. "I think I know how you feel," she said. "That was a terrible day for me as well...." She told the woman how she also had been on the streetcar and how her father and Mrs. Scott had drowned.

"Dear girl." She touched Rose's hand briefly and softly. "We have both lost the people closest to our hearts. But tell me, what has happened to you since then? Who cares for you now?"

Rose explained about Aunt Ellen and the attic room at the O'Reillys'.

"Yes, I know the family. Their daughter Kathleen is about the same age as my Allison was," the old woman said with a heavy sigh. She seemed to be on the verge of tears again.

Rose struggled to think of something that might take the woman's mind off the accident. What could she say? Something. Anything.

"The O'Reillys have been very kind to us, putting us up and all. Miss Kathleen let me visit her in her room. She has a wardrobe full of dresses. I am sure she could wear a different dress every day of the month and there'd still be some left over. Not only that. She will be going away on a trip soon and when she's in London she says she is going to buy more clothes." Rose chattered on and on. Her words sounded frivolous, even to her own ears.

But despite this, the woman appeared to be listening. Something seemed to relax in her manner; it was hard to say exactly what. To look at her, nothing had changed. But she seemed calmer now and she had regained her composure. She dabbed her eyes, straightened her shoulders and said, "How lovely. Pardon me. I've just realized we haven't introduced ourselves." She offered her hand. "Mrs. Ida Cameron. I am very pleased to make your acquaintance."

Rose took Mrs. Cameron's hand. "My name is Rose Laurie, but you can call me Rose. And I'm happy to meet you."

"Do you think, perhaps, we could talk again sometime?" Mrs. Cameron asked.

"Of course. I'd like that very much."

"Will you be here tomorrow afternoon?"

"I come here almost every afternoon after my chores. I'll look for you tomorrow then."

It was mid-afternoon. The air shimmered in the heat. Rose sat in the shade of an arbutus tree, describing

Aunt Ellen and the O'Reillys' household. Mrs. Cameron listened and nodded her head. Rose could see Mrs. Cameron's face had lost some of its sadness. She smiled more often. Occasionally she even laughed out loud. She had started eating regular meals in the last few weeks, her colour had improved and the hollows in her cheeks had softened.

But when Rose offered to take her up to the house, she shook her head. "I'm sorry, Rose. I don't feel up to being with other people yet. It's still too soon. I do like being with you though. You're like a tonic to me."

They watched the workmen at the new bridge. The construction site was very close to the ruin of the old bridge. The men busied themselves with their gear and workhorses. Massive piles of timber and white stone blocks had been piled in readiness on the banks of the shore.

"What a big job it will be. Building a whole new bridge and not just repairing the old one," Rose commented.

"It surely is. It's a tremendous undertaking," agreed Mrs. Cameron. "But sometimes it's better to make a new beginning. And I suppose this is one of those times."

Rose was glad they were in the shade out of the glare of the sun. A comfortable silence settled between them, a silence that neither felt the need to fill. And when Rose did say something, Mrs. Cameron would always listen with interest. She never corrected her grammar or told her not to use slang, the way some older people did.

"I'll tell you a funny thing," Rose said, after a while. "When I first saw you, I thought you were a ghost. Everyone was talking about a ghost—all in black, by the bridge—and so I thought it was you."

Mrs. Cameron laughed. "Did you? Imagine being mistaken for a ghost? I must have looked a sight. Well, I have a confidence to share as well. There were many times I would watch you, when you didn't know I was there. You looked like such a lovely girl. I would see you walking on the beach, and after a while I found myself wondering more and more about you. Who you were. What you were doing here."

"I'll tell you what I was doing," Rose said. "I was looking for my locket. It was my first piece of jewellery. It had been my mother's. But I lost it the day of the accident at the bridge. I remember the last time I saw it. I was on the streetcar and I looked down and it was shining in the sunlight. Then, after the accident, after I had been pulled ashore, I realized it was gone. And ever since, I've searched and searched, but I've never found it. In fact, it turned out...well, I'm ashamed to tell you."

"What is it, Rose?"

"I even come here at night to search for my locket. But at night, I'm sleepwalking. That's what Aunt Ellen tells me. She's seen me do it. She saw me returning to the house one night. I didn't know anything about it until she told me. Other people have seen me as well but they think I am a ghost. That's the strange thing. The ghost by the bridge...is me!"

Mrs. Cameron looked shocked. "Dear child!"

"Now, at night, Aunt Ellen has taken to leaving a

chair in front of the door of our room, as a precaution. She says if I go sleepwalking again, I would have to move the chair to get out of the room, and that might wake her up. Then she could stop me from going." Rose paused. "You're the only person, besides Aunt Ellen, who knows of this. We haven't told anyone else."

"Isn't it strange?" Mrs. Cameron said thoughtfully. "We've both been mistaken for ghosts. That's something else we have in common then." Mrs. Cameron was silent for a moment. "You know, Rose, this business about the sleepwalking...I don't think it's anything to be ashamed of. In fact, I think it's quite understandable. Of course you want to find your locket. It's only natural. I think if I was in your circumstances I would be sleepwalking too. And you needn't worry, I won't tell anyone. Your secret is safe with me.

"Now tell me, Rose, there is something I've always wondered. When I used to see you here, before we met, you would sit at that log, near the bank." She pointed across the beach. "It looked almost as if you were pretending to play the piano."

"I was," Rose jumped up excitedly. "Come with me. I'll show you."

They crossed the rocky beach and Rose ran her fingers over the lines etched into the soft wood of the log. "Do you see how I've marked it? It's a keyboard. I can play my music here without disturbing anyone. It's not like a real piano, of course, but I can imagine the music in my head."

"But surely the O'Reillys would let you play their

piano. They do have a piano, don't they?"

"They have two pianos! But I mustn't make any noise or touch anything on the O'Reillys' side of the house. My place is on the servants' side. Aunt Ellen explained all the rules on the first day."

"But, Rose, I'm sure if you asked the O'Reillys, they would happily give you permission to play."

Rose felt a prickling of guilt as she remembered Mr. Norman catching her at the drawing-room piano.

"I couldn't ask them. Aunt Ellen says we mustn't impose. The O'Reillys have been very kind to us, but we've already stayed too long and we have to find our own place. Aunt Ellen has been all over town looking at boarding houses."

"Perhaps she'll find a boarding house with a piano."

"I hope so," Rose said doubtfully. "Aunt Ellen says it's hard to find a suitable boarding house on her salary. I know it's a lot harder now that she has me to think about as well."

There was a distant shout from the workmen at the new bridge. A team of horses were dragging another load of timbers down the road to the construction site. Rose and Mrs. Cameron watched the activity, both quiet for a moment.

"Do you know what I wish?" Rose said. "I can just close my eyes and picture this. Aunt Ellen and I would have a place of our own with a piano that I could play whenever I wanted. And Aunt Ellen wouldn't have to be a parlourmaid anymore. She'd be a seamstress and have her own sewing machine. She'd make dresses for ladies—lovely, fashionable dresses.

That's how I imagine it. That's all we would need—nothing fancy. We'd be as happy as could be."

⚜

Jess jumped. Somewhere a phone was ringing.

She looked around in a daze. She was in Rose's room in the attic.

Libby's voice floated up through the open window. "Hello? Yes, that's fine, Louisa."

Jess tried to peer down but she could only see the roofline and the tops of the trees. Libby must be talking on a cellphone. Her voice continued. "I have room for one more tea at two o'clock. By the way, have you seen Jess?" Then Libby's voice faded. She must be walking away.

Jess closed the window. She rushed downstairs, banged through the screen door and ran down the gravel path to catch up with Libby.

"There you are, Jess!" Libby turned around. "I was wondering where you'd got to."

"I was just...." Oh no. What should she say? "I was just doing a little research on the history of the house." She said finally. In a way, her answer was not so far from the truth.

"I don't think I know anyone who's as keen on history as you are," Libby said with a look of approval. "Now...we're missing some croquet balls. Would you mind looking through the bushes at the edge of the lawn? They must be in there somewhere."

"Sure, Libby. I'll find them."

Jess poked around in the bushes, reaching far back through the branches and leaves to retrieve the balls,

165

but the whole time she thought about Rose. What had happened to Rose after Point Ellice House?

The question was still running through her mind as she walked home later in the day. Then she suddenly stopped. Some of the people from Rose's time would have had children. And some of those families may still be living in Victoria.

Jess ran the rest of the way home. She grabbed the phone book and the portable phone from the hall table and raced up the stairs to her room.

When Rose had met Mrs. Cameron, she'd introduced herself as Rose Laurie. But Laurie might not have been her last name. It could have been her middle name. Jess thumbed through the pages and ran her finger down the columns. Laughton. Laurel. Laurie! There were only a few Lauries.

But if Rose had a family, that meant she would have been married. Her last name would have changed.

Her eyes fell on Cynthia Abbott's diary on the bedside table. Quickly she flipped back to the A's in the phone book. Cynthia might have married and changed her name, but not her brother. Francis would have kept the Abbott name. She scanned the columns. There had to be forty or fifty Abbotts.

She dialled the first number. As she listened to it ring she smiled. Only a few months ago she never would have phoned someone up, someone she didn't know, and ask to talk about their family history.

"Oh, hello," she said when a voice on the other

166

end answered. "You don't know me, but I'm trying to find the family of Cynthia and Francis Abbott. They lived in Victoria about a hundred years ago. Have you ever heard of them? Cynthia and Francis Abbott?...No? Okay. Thanks anyway."

She worked methodically down the list, crossing off numbers as she went and making notes of the ones where she couldn't get through. It was slow progress. After a while her stomach began to rumble. It must be almost suppertime.

"Hello?" A woman's voice.

"Oh! Hello. My name is Jess and I'm trying to track down some of the Abbott family. Cynthia and Francis Abbott."

"Oh, yes. I know who you mean."

"You do?"

"Yes. I'm married to Francis Abbott's son. Francis died...oh, let me think...it would be twenty-five years ago. What was your interest in him?"

"Well I was interested in both Francis and Cynthia. You see...I found Cynthia Abbott's diary, the diary she wrote when she was a girl. It was hidden behind the wainscotting in my room."

There was a sharp intake of breath on the other end of the line.

"Cynthia's diary!"

13

CYNTHIA'S REVENGE

The next morning Jess found herself fidgeting on the Abbotts' couch. The couple were taking a leisurely look through Cynthia's diary. Jess studied Mr. Abbott's white hair and thickened fingers. It surprised her to see how old he was. She'd been expecting someone younger. How strange to think that the Francis she knew as a boy would have a son who was an old man now.

"What an interesting find!" Mr. Abbott said. "You say it was wedged behind the wainscotting. Amazing! What a devious girl that Cynthia was. Of course, I knew her many years after she wrote this. She was my Aunt Cynthia. She used to come over to our house for Sunday dinners when I was a boy. She was a spinster her whole life. Never married. And it wasn't surprising. She kept to herself for the most part. And she always seemed irritable. She'd spend the whole Sunday dinner arguing with my father. He'd say one thing and she'd contradict him. He'd say the sky was blue and she'd say it was grey. I was a little afraid of her, if the truth be told.

"Sometimes I'd see her walking around town. She'd always wear the same old coat, I remember—dark brown wool and buttoned up to her neck, even on the hottest days in summer.

"When she died—and it's many years ago now—we went through all her things. Her last home was an apartment above a butcher shop. You had to go around the back of the shop, into an alley and up some rickety stairs. And when you opened the door—my word!—it was crammed with stuff. Everywhere! Piled almost up to the ceiling. There was hardly room to move, just little pathways from room to room. Newspapers, milk bottles—most of it junk. Practically nothing worth saving. It was a real fire trap if ever there was one."

Jess sat forward eagerly. "When you were looking through Cynthia's things, did you find any jewellery?"

"Jewellery?"

"Yes. Did you find a silver, oval-shaped locket?

169

Cynthia talks about it in her diary."

"A locket? Mmmmm. Let me think." He glanced at his wife.

Mrs. Abbott shrugged her shoulders. "I don't recall a locket. But I can get her jewellery box and we'll have a look." She ambled slowly down the hallway and eventually returned, carrying a Chinese black lacquered box decorated with painted trees and birds.

Jess froze. It was exactly as she had pictured it. It had to be the same Chinese box Cynthia had been given for her birthday, the box where she'd hidden the locket.

"Well, let's see if it's here," said Mrs. Abbott, and she set the box down on the coffee table in front of them. Jess leaned forward as the old woman opened the first drawer. Inside they found a maple leaf brooch, a clunky necklace of red and white beads, and a ring with the stone missing. She opened the next drawer and rummaged through the tangled spaghetti of knotted chains. No locket. The third drawer was filled with cheap costume jewellery as well. Finally, she opened the last drawer, poked her finger through and shook her head.

"Sorry, Jess. I'm afraid there's no locket."

Jess slumped back into the couch. But then she jumped up. "Mr. Abbott, there's a poem in the diary. Something about the secret of the jewellery box. It was an entry in the summer, on Cynthia's birthday." Jess hung over his shoulder as he skipped ahead to the right page.

"Ah. Here it is. This is the part." He cleared his throat and then read aloud in a deep, dramatic voice,

"One, two, three, four,
A little treasure in every drawer.
But you must find the secret key
To unlock the jewel box mystery."

Jess quickly snatched up the Chinese box. There was no keyhole.

Mrs. Abbott gave Jess' shoulder a sympathetic pat. "What a shame. I'm afraid it's not the right jewellery box. You're looking for one with a lock and a key. You must be disappointed, dear. I'm sorry."

"I *am* disappointed," Jess admitted. "I thought for sure it was going to be the right one." She might as well admit it. She was no closer to finding the locket than before. "Well, I guess that's it then." She stood up. "I'd better be going now. They'll be expecting me at Point Ellice House."

"So soon? But we haven't finished looking through the diary yet," Mrs. Abbott said.

"Why don't you keep it for a few days?" Jess offered. "I could come back and pick it up another day."

Mrs. Abbott saw Jess to the door. "Thank you for coming, Jess. And thank you for letting us borrow the diary."

Jess took the bus to Point Ellice House and found Libby in the kitchen.

"Morning, Jess. I'm glad you're here. Could you take the lemon loaf out of the oven when the timer rings? I want to get back to the garden and do a bit more weeding before it gets too hot."

"Okay, Libby. Don't worry. I'll keep an eye on it."

Jess watched Libby walk down the path around the far corner of the house. Then she turned back to

171

the kitchen. No one else was there. Just as she was considering sneaking a cookie off one of the trays, the muscles in her neck and spine tightened. She shivered with anticipation.

Rose stood nervously at Mrs. Cameron's door, wondering if she should knock or pull the doorbell. Mrs. Cameron had invited her to come for the afternoon and play her piano. But when Rose arrived at the address, she was astounded to find it was no ordinary house. She double-checked the address but there was no mistake. The number was correct. The house could only properly be called a mansion—a mansion with turrets and gables and bristling with chimney pots. Up until that moment Rose had no idea that Mrs. Cameron lived in such a grand house, far bigger than the O'Reillys' house. She rang the doorbell. Thank goodness she had taken the time to tidy her hair back with a ribbon. And her dress was washed and neatly pressed.

A maid opened the door.

"Good afternoon. My name is Rose. I'm here to see Mrs. Cameron," Rose said, thinking she would be told she had the wrong house.

But the maid welcomed her in. "Oh yes. Mrs. Cameron has been expecting you. Come this way please."

Rose followed behind, wondering if perhaps Mrs. Cameron was a housekeeper with a modest room in the back of the house. But no, the maid was escorting her through an impressive front hall and into the drawing-room.

Mrs. Cameron sat on plush, green velvet sofa, sipping a cup of tea. Her face brightened when she saw Rose.

"Oh, Rose! I'm so happy you came," she greeted her warmly. "Please sit down."

Rose waited until the maid had left the room and then she couldn't help but say, "I didn't know you lived in a mansion! Why didn't you tell me? All this time we've known each other, and I thought you were no different from Aunt Ellen and me."

Mrs. Cameron laughed. "I am no different from you and your Aunt Ellen. It just happens that I live in a big house, that's all. Quite honestly, I don't think about it very much. When all is said and done, money is of very little importance. That is something I've learned over the years. And there's been a good number of years at that! Now, would you like some tea? There's Indian and Oolong."

But Rose did not answer. She had just noticed—positioned in the centre of a wide sweep of bay windows on the far side of the drawing-room—a magnificent, black and gleaming grand piano.

Mrs. Cameron followed her gaze. "Or perhaps you would like to play the piano first," she suggested.

Rose nodded mutely, hardly daring to speak. She had never seen such a fine instrument. Her fingers trembled as she approached the bench. She sat down, marvelling at the row of smooth black and white keys. Real keys! Then she played a song she'd memorized at Mrs. Scott's house a long time ago, simple but beautiful. She sounded the last note and savoured the sound as it faded away.

"Very nice, Rose. Please play another," said Mrs. Cameron.

Rose opened a piece of sheet music that was on the stand in front of her. It was a piece she had never played before. She worked her way through it, practising the more difficult sections over and over until they flowed smoothly.

When she finished, Mrs. Cameron said, "My daughter Allison used to play that song. It was one of her favourites."

"It's lovely," said Rose. She turned around. "I didn't know your daughter used to play the piano."

"Oh yes. But no one has played it since the accident."

"But don't you play?" Rose asked.

"Me?" Mrs. Cameron looked surprised. "I never learned how to play."

"But you could learn. I could teach you." Rose stood up excitedly.

Mrs. Cameron looked flustered. "I don't know, Rose. I can't imagine I'd be much of a musician. And besides, I'm certainly too old to learn now."

"But I can see you love music. You have such a beautiful piano and you have me to show you how." Rose took Mrs. Cameron firmly by the hand and led her to the piano bench.

Mrs. Cameron sat down. "I don't really think I can do this, Rose," she said, half laughing, half serious.

Rose ignored her protests. "Now, put your fingers on the keys with your thumb on this note." She lay her hands on the keyboard and Mrs. Cameron obediently did the same.

"Play one finger at a time, like this." Rose played one note after another in quick succession. Mrs. Cameron followed suit, slower, hesitating at each note.

"Good. Now try this."

The lesson continued with Rose demonstrating, Mrs. Cameron watching intently and then doing her best to do the same.

"See?" Rose said after Mrs. Cameron had stumbled through a simple exercise. "You can play the piano. You're doing very well for your first time. You should practise what we did today, and I'll teach you more another time."

"Goodness. Who would have thought I'd be learning to play the piano at my age?" Mrs. Cameron sounded genuinely amazed. She went back to her green velvet sofa, looking very pleased with herself and settled down to listen again as Rose played.

When it was time for Rose to go, Mrs. Cameron said, "I can't thank you enough for the lesson, Rose. And for your lovely playing. The piano is here for you any time you'd like to play. Every day, if you'd like."

Rose hurried out of the chicken house with a basket full of eggs. They were still warm, each a perfect oval, but some were caked with bits of straw and muck. She would clean them up, and she'd still have time to go to Mrs. Cameron's to play the piano. But at that moment a carriage pulled up in the gravel driveway and stopped at the front door. When Rose saw who it was she wanted to run back to the chicken house and hide. But it was too late. Cynthia and

Francis Abbott had already seen her.

Francis waved, called out her name and jumped down from the carriage. Cynthia, meanwhile, remained in her seat and twirled her parasol impatiently.

"Rose! How's the pig?" said Francis.

Rose felt her cheeks flush as she remembered that disgraceful day. "The pig is fine, but I feel terrible about what happened. It was all my fault," she admitted. She cast a wary eye in Cynthia's direction. "I truly am very sorry."

Cynthia did not appear to take any notice of the apology but Francis grinned good-naturedly. "Don't say that! I thought it was wonderful. I really enjoyed myself. But never mind. Look what I found...." He was digging into a pocket of his knee pants. "It was right here...," he said, now looking in the other pocket. "Oh, blast it! Where is it now? Maybe I left it in my jacket."

"Left what?"

"Your locket!"

Rose clasped her hands together with surprise. She could hardly believe her ears.

"I found it when I was down at the bridge. It was in a pile of old timber. But where did I put it now?" He ran back to the carriage. "Cynthia, pass me my jacket, will you? I must have left the locket in my jacket."

"For goodness sake, Francis. Can't you remember anything?" She tossed the jacket unceremoniously off the bench.

Francis searched through each of the pockets, pulling them completely inside out and becoming more and more distressed.

"Maybe it fell out in the carriage," he said. He poked his head under the seat. "Help me look, Cynthia. It's got to be here somewhere."

Cynthia made the merest effort to look, inclining her head slightly to the left and then to the right. "What a shame. It looks like it's lost again," she said with an overly sweet smile. "Well, come along, Francis darling. We should be getting home."

"I'm sorry, Rose." Francis stood up and shrugged his shoulders. "I wanted to surprise you. I can't think what's happened to it. Maybe it slipped out of my pocket when I was at the Grants'."

Rose felt her heart sink with disappointment. "It will probably show up again," she said, trying to sound hopeful.

"I'm sure it will. And when it does, I'll bring it straight over to you."

"Say goodbye, Francis," Cynthia said, letting her eye fall on Rose's basket of unwashed eggs and wrinkling her nose. "The girl should be getting back to her chores."

Rose's feet felt heavy as she trudged into the scullery. Imagine! Coming so close to having her locket returned and then losing it again. She filled a basin with clear, cold water, plunged the eggs in, one by one, and carefully scrubbed them with a soft brush. Just as she was putting them into the larder, Aunt Ellen came into the kitchen.

"Rose! The O'Reillys are asking for you." She looked anxious. "They're in the drawing-room. I don't know what it's about. You haven't been up to anything

177

else, have you?"

Rose gulped. "No...I don't think so." Why would the O'Reillys be summoning her into the drawing-room?

Aunt Ellen followed her nervously down the hall and past the red baize door. Then, at the entrance to the drawing-room, Rose stopped short. There before her, all having tea, were Mr. and Mrs. O'Reilly, Miss Kathleen, Jack who was just home from work and—Rose's eyes opened wide with surprise—Mrs. Cameron.

"Come in, Rose," Mrs. O'Reilly said. "And Ellen, please do come in and sit down as well."

Rose found a chair near the door. How peculiar to be asked to join them. What could it mean?

"Mrs. Cameron, I believe you know Rose." Mrs. O'Reilly made the introductions. "And this is Rose's Aunt Ellen."

Mrs. Cameron smiled as she acknowledged Rose. Then she turned to Aunt Ellen. "A pleasure to finally meet you, Ellen. Rose has told me so much about you. I've come to make a rather unusual proposal." She took a sip of tea and cleared her throat. "Although I'm afraid it will put the O'Reillys in a difficult spot. You see, I would like to offer you a position as a parlourmaid in my house. At the moment I have one girl who does all the cooking and cleaning. She has been trained as a cook and that is what she prefers to do. She is only filling in with the rest as a favour to me. So I've been looking for a second girl. The O'Reillys tell me they are very satisfied with your work, Ellen. They've given you an excellent recommendation.

Would you be interested in coming to work for me?"

Aunt Ellen blinked. "But I've promised to be in service here at the O'Reillys'. It wouldn't be right to leave them."

"Don't worry about us," Mrs. O'Reilly assured her. "Mrs. Cameron and I have already discussed it, and we've agreed it would be the best thing for you and Rose. We'll put an advertisement in the newspaper today to fill your position here, and then you'll be free to go."

"With all our best wishes," added Mr. O'Reilly. "And I must say it sounds like Mrs. Cameron's offer will suit you very well."

Mrs. Cameron nodded. "I can match your current salary and add a little more as an incentive. I can also provide living quarters for both you and Rose. I have two very nice bedrooms in the back of the house, overlooking the garden. One for you and one for Rose. There is a little sitting room between them for you both to share, very cozy and comfortably furnished. I think it will be to your liking. The piano in the drawing-room, of course, will be for Rose to play as she wishes." She looked toward Rose and smiled then turned her attention back to Aunt Ellen. "So, would you be interested in such an offer?"

Rose held her breath. Say yes. Oh, please say yes, she wanted to say. But she knew better than to speak out of turn. Instead, she made herself sit very still and tucked her hands tightly under her knees to contain herself.

Aunt Ellen lifted her chin. "But surely this is too generous. Not only will you increase my wage, but you will provide living quarters for us both? You are very kind, Mrs. Cameron, but I'm not sure it would do for me. You see, I don't want any favours. I've always believed in earning my keep."

Rose couldn't believe her ears. Here was the solution to all their problems and Aunt Ellen was saying no.

"From my point of view, it is a fair arrangement for us both," insisted Mrs. Cameron. "You will be working to earn your keep. I will have secured good, reliable help and—this is something I've been looking forward to—I will have Rose to fill the house with music and to give me a lesson now and again." She eyed Aunt Ellen hopefully and then added, "And, if I understand correctly from Rose, you are interested in doing some seamstress work, Ellen?"

Aunt Ellen nodded and her proud expression softened just a little.

"I have a sewing machine and I would be grateful if you would do a bit of sewing for me. I have one or two things that need altering at the moment. I'm thinking I might like to have a new skirt made as well. We could see how you do and if your work is good I would be happy to refer my friends to you. What do you say?"

Aunt Ellen hesitated and then looked at Rose. "Rose, what do you think?"

"I think you should accept! It sounds perfect." Her hands flew out from under her knees in her eagerness, but she quickly tucked them back under again.

Aunt Ellen turned back to Mrs. Cameron. "Well, if it suits Rose, it suits me. I say yes. I'll do it."

Mrs. Cameron clasped her hands together happily. "Good! I'm so glad. You can move in whenever you're ready. And Rose will be all settled in by the time school starts in September. We'll have to make sure she gets some new school clothes. And a piano teacher...would you like a piano teacher, Rose?"

"Oh, yes!" Rose said at once but then immediately bit her tongue. A piano teacher would be far too expensive for Aunt Ellen.

"I'll see what I can arrange. Now please don't worry about paying for it, Ellen. It's something I want to do for Rose in return for all the kindness she's shown me."

"Kindness? Me?" Rose asked. What could she be talking about? It was Mrs. Cameron who was so kind to *her*.

Mrs. Cameron smiled gently. "When I was miserable and sick, you helped me. You didn't know then whether I was wealthy or poor. If I had been a penniless wretch, I have no doubt you would have treated me the same way. You spent your money to buy food for me. I'll always remember how you ran up to that man at the bridge—without a moment's hesitation—and then came running back with something for me to eat.

"And that's not all," Mrs. Cameron continued. "You've helped me through the most difficult time in my life. You made me laugh and enjoy things again when I didn't think such a thing was possible. And now, when I wake up in the morning, I look forward to each day. I have you to thank for that, Rose. That is why I want you to come and live with me."

Each of the O'Reillys turned to regard Rose with the same expression, eyes intent and eyebrows raised.

"Compassion and spirit," Mr. O'Reilly said, thoughtfully. "Certainly traits to admire."

Rose felt her cheeks flush and she looked down at her lap. She knew very well a young lady must remain polite and decorous. But such a joyfulness rose inside her that she could not contain herself a moment longer. In the next instant she leapt up from her chair. She threw her arms around Mrs. Cameron and cried out, "Thank you! Thank you for everything."

Mrs. Cameron laughed happily and hugged her back.

"I'm sure you will find Ellen and Rose a very pleasant addition to your home," Mrs. O'Reilly said, looking on.

"Yes," chipped in Jack with a twinkle in his eye. "And if you keep any animals or livestock—such as *pigs*, you can be sure Rose will see to it that they get plenty of exercise."

So! Jack must have heard about Daisy's escape and the disastrous birthday party. Rose could see Mrs. Cameron looking perplexed and opening her mouth to ask what he meant by the remark.

Fortunately Miss Kathleen chose that moment to stand up and say, "I know we will all be very sorry to see you both go. There's something I'd like to present to Rose as a going-away gift. I was intending to give it to you when I left on my trip, but I think perhaps now would be a more appropriate time. Do you remember the yellow rose you'd admired in the garden? I said I would paint a picture of it for you.

Well, I've finished it." She went next door and brought back the painting, saying, "You can hang it in your new room."

Miss Kathleen had done the petals in Rose's favourite shade of yellow—not too bright but still cheerful, like soft sunshine. Rose peered closely and in the bottom corner, written in tiny letters she could only just read, was an inscription, A Rose for a Rose. K. O'Reilly, 1896.

Rose was delighted. "Miss Kathleen, it's beautiful. Thank you. Whenever I look at it I'll remember the summer I spent here."

"I'll remember you too. And I promise to send you pretty postcards from all the places I visit on my travels."

Mrs. O'Reilly put down her teacup. "Rose, I must say. I didn't realize until now that you were such an avid musician. I'm sorry we didn't offer the piano for you to play before. But perhaps you could play something for us now. If you would? I think we would all enjoy it."

Rose was happy to oblige. She sat down on the bench, positioned her hands over the keys and played the first note.

EEEEEEEEEE...

Jess started. What was that? A strange note from the piano? No. She was in the Point Ellice kitchen and a lovely, warm baking smell filled the air.

The lemon loaf.

And Libby's kitchen timer had just gone off.

14

THE SECRET KEY

Jess slid into bed, pulled up the covers and drifted off into a lovely, warm sleep. It was hard to say how long she had been asleep when suddenly her eyes flew open and she bolted straight up in bed.

The key! She'd been looking for a key. The jewellery box key!

The poem from Cynthia's diary rang as clearly in her mind as if she had just read it.

"One, two, three, four,
   A little treasure in every drawer.
   But you must find the secret key
   To unlock the jewel box mystery."
   She lay back down, but her heart was hammering in her chest. It was a long time before she could get to sleep again.

The next morning Jess sat, once again, on the Abbotts' couch. The Abbotts settled themselves across from her as she explained. "The key to the jewellery box that we read about in the poem...it might not be a real key that you can hold in your hand. It might just mean the answer to a puzzle. So the Chinese jewellery box might be the right box after all."

Mrs. Abbott looked doubtful. "I think we had a good look at the box yesterday. I can't imagine we missed anything. But you're welcome to have another look if you'd like." She set the painted jewellery box down on the coffee table in front of Jess.

Jess studied the Chinese box. What could the secret key be? Was there a clue in the painted birds or trees? She examined them closely. The tiny details had been painted with a fine brush, but there was nothing about them that seemed out of place—no hidden clues that she could see. She picked the box up and held it high above her head, checking the smooth, glossy black lacquered surface underneath. She turned it over. Could the top of the box lift up? Had it been glued shut? She looked carefully to see if there was a join in the wood. But there was nothing. She tried to twist each gold drawer knob, checking for any movement. Nothing. Then she pulled the drawers out and examined their red satin linings before laying them down on the coffee table. She looked inside. Just black paint.

Perhaps she'd been wrong after all. There seemed to be nothing unusual about it—just a box with four drawers and no secrets to hide.

She picked up one of the drawers to slide it back in. Then she stopped. Why was this drawer longer than the one beside it? She laid them side by side. It was definitely longer.

"Look!" she said. She lined all four drawers up in a row. There were two long drawers and two short ones. "They're different sizes. There has to be a reason why they're different sizes."

She picked the box up again and peered into the black interior, angling it so the light was better. The box was constructed so that the long drawers went in at the top and the shorter drawers slid into the bottom. There was something blocking the back, some sort of barrier to prevent the bottom drawers from sliding in too far.

Then she had an idea. She turned the box upside down. There was a quick, sharp *click* from inside the box. She felt it through her hands as much as heard it. Something had shifted within the box.

Mr. and Mrs. Abbott had heard it too. A hush fell over the room and all eyes were on the box.

Jess said a silent prayer to herself. Then she peered down into the box. Inside, against the back of the box, a secret drawer had slid open. It had appeared from behind the bottom drawer barrier.

"What is it?" Mrs. Abbott asked. "What do you see?"

"It's a secret drawer," Jess said, hardly believing it herself. "It can only open when the other drawers are removed."

And there was something in the secret drawer, something hard to see. She tilted the box. A small parcel, wrapped in a bit of fabric, dropped onto her lap.

They all gasped.

The wrapping had probably once been a snowy-white cotton, but it was now yellowed with age. It was tied together with a length of faded lavender ribbon. Jess' fingers fumbled as she struggled to loosen the knot. Then, at last, it came free. She pulled open the fabric.

Inside, as beautiful as any treasure, lay Rose's locket.

Jess laughed out loud at the sight of it. Then her eyes misted with tears. She picked it up and held its smooth, oval shape in her palm. How finely painted the feathery design of flowers and leaves were! She held it up to the light, but the silver was no longer shiny. It had tarnished and dulled over the years. The chain dangled through her fingers, and there it was—the link that had broken in the accident. Jess could picture the chain slipping away from Rose's neck and the locket lying amongst the wreckage of the bridge. She could picture Francis pulling it out from between two pieces of timber. And then Cynthia...she could imagine Cynthia's sly hand slipping it from his pocket and hiding it away in the jewellery box.

Jess looked down at the old locket cupped in her hand. "It's just the way I thought it would be," she said, her voice barely a whisper.

"How do you know it's the right locket, Jess?" Mrs. Abbott asked.

Jess had no doubt. "Watch. When I open it up, inside it will say, Courage."

She opened the locket, and there, indeed, written in beautiful curling script, was the word Courage.

Mrs. Abbott looked puzzled. "Jess? How did you know what would be written inside? I don't remember Cynthia writing in her diary that it said Courage. She wrote that there was an inscription but she doesn't say what it was."

Jess swallowed hard. The Abbotts were both looking at her, waiting for an explanation. What could she say? The truth seemed too impossible to believe.

"Well...umm...I've been volunteering at Point Ellice House this summer. I had to do a lot of reading about the people who lived there...and um...."

Mrs. Abbott jumped in. "And you read about the servant girl who stayed at Point Ellice House, the one Cynthia talks about in her diary?"

"Uh...yes." Jess said, happy to agree with any plausible explanation. "I read about her in one of their history binders. Her name was Rose Laurie and she was in the streetcar accident on the bridge. That's when she lost her locket."

"So that's how you knew about the locket—that it said Courage. What a lot of detail their history binders must have!" Mrs. Abbott shook her head in amazement.

"Oh, yes. They have all sorts of information," Jess continued quickly. "And after the accident she lived with her aunt who was the parlourmaid at Point Ellice House. And then later they both went to live with a Mrs. Cameron. There was no more information about what happened to them later."

There was a moment of silence in the room.

Mr. Abbott cleared his throat. "Cameron? Cameron you say?"

Jess nodded.

"Now, I wonder..." Mr. Abbott scratched his head slowly. "I wonder if I might be able to shed a little light on the matter. You see, it's just occurred to me who this Rose might be. I knew of a lady by the name of Rose McBride. Of course that would have been her married name—not Rose Laurie. Do you suppose it could be the same person?"

Jess sat forward. "Maybe. What do you remember about her?"

He crossed his arms comfortably over his stomach. "When I was a young boy, I remember a Mrs. Rose McBride who lived over in the James Bay area of the city. Near the park and not too far from the water. A big Victorian house it was, with turrets and verandas. It was known as the old Cameron Mansion. That's what people called it because it had been built for the Cameron family a long time before I was born. Now, if we're talking about the same people...the same Rose and Mrs. Cameron you referred to...."

Jess swallowed. "Did this Rose play the piano?"

"Well, yes, she did as a matter of fact. She gave lessons."

Jess felt goosebumps spring up on her arms. "It has to be the same Rose then," she said. "It's too much of a coincidence not to be."

Mr. Abbott nodded. "Well, I'm thinking that Mrs. Cameron must have willed her estate to Rose. That's my guess anyway. I remember Mrs. Rose McBride living there. And a few of my friends used to go to her house for piano lessons. She always gave them cookies after their lessons and she liked to laugh as much as any of them.

"If I'd been musical, I'd probably have taken lessons from her too. But I don't have a musical bone in my body. No one in my family does. We're practically tone deaf, the lot of us.

"But Mrs. McBride was a fine pianist. And she taught the piano because she loved it, not because she needed the money. She had a husband and a couple of children. And she lived to be a good old age. But it's been years now since she died. Thirty maybe. Could be longer. The old mansion isn't there anymore either. It was torn down and they built apartment buildings on the property. Her children and grandchildren moved back east. Ontario, I believe.

"Yes. It was another era. But it's all changed now I'm afraid," said Mr. Abbott, shaking his head sadly.

"Do you know if Rose ever gave piano recitals?" Jess asked, thinking back to the day so many years ago when Rose realized that was what she wanted to do.

"Piano recitals? Yes, it seems to me she did," Mr.

Abbott answered. He pointed to the jewellery box with his cane. "Would you mind passing me the box? I wouldn't mind having a look at this secret drawer."

He turned the box upside down and back again to make the secret drawer appear and then disappear. "You're a very clever girl, Jess. If it wasn't for you, this drawer would have remained a secret forever. Do you know what I think?"

Jess shook her head.

"With all the trouble you went to to find this locket, I think you should have it. I'm sure we both agree," He glanced at Mrs. Abbott and she nodded her head. "The locket rightfully belongs to you, Jess."

15

COURAGE

Jess stood alone in the gathering darkness underneath the bridge. The summer had slipped away as quickly as sand trickling through her fingers. Hardly more than a fleeting moment, and it had gone. Now, as she looked around her, she could see the first hints of autumn—the shock of yellow on the trees and a crispness to the air that reminded her of biting into an apple. The days were shorter, and nighttime was coming earlier.

Tomorrow would be her last day volunteering at Point Ellice House. And the day after that would be the first day of school. Her heart gave a little flutter at the thought. Things are going to be fine at school this year, she told herself firmly. And, this time, she really believed it. She had a feeling it was going to be a good year.

But she was sorry that Point Ellice House was closing for the season. She was going to miss it. Every room in the house and every part of the garden held memories...of her own summer there, of course, but also of the time Rose had spent there. There was the sink in the scullery where Rose washed the eggs, the door that lead to the attic, the piano in the drawing-room and the little grey and white porcelain pig in Miss Kathleen's room that looked so much like Daisy.

Jess looked down at the silver locket she held in her hand. It had been weeks since she'd found it. And in that entire time, there had been no sign of Rose. No more visions and an empty feeling inside, as if Rose had gone. Jess had polished the locket, and taken it to a jeweller to repair the chain, but somehow she could not bring herself to wear it. It still felt as if it belonged to Rose.

Jess stared across the water, trying to focus all her concentration.

"Please come back, Rose. Please," she whispered. "I have your locket. I found it for you."

She strained her eyes across the Gorge toward Point Ellice House and waited, shivering, in the shadows of the bridge. The air felt heavy with dampness. Her breath hung like a white cloud before her. The minutes ticked by but nothing happened.

Jess pulled her sweater closer against the chill. The cars on the bridge rumbled overhead. The water lapped along the shore. And the evening slowly darkened.

Still nothing happened.

Perhaps Rose was not going to appear. Perhaps there was no need. Now that her locket had been found, Rose's search may have come to an end.

Jess waited a few more minutes, just to be sure. But no light appeared. She clasped her fingers tightly around the locket and swallowed hard. "Goodbye, Rose," she whispered, finally, into the darkness.

Early the next morning Jess fastened the locket's clasp behind her neck and checked the mirror. Her reflection looked squarely back at her, and the locket gleamed against her shirt. It suited her, she decided. And, although nothing had happened last night under the bridge, somehow it felt as if the locket belonged to her now. She knew she would wear it proudly. It would always remind her of Rose.

Jess' eye moved up to her hair. As usual, one or two strands had escaped from her ponytail. But when Jess reached up, instead of trying to smooth them back into place, she loosened a few more curls and grinned at herself in the mirror.

She turned and looked around her room with satisfaction. It was finally finished and her dad was right—it *had* been worth it. All the mess and the dust had been cleared away. It didn't look like Cynthia's room anymore. Now it was open and airy with lots of light. There was new wallpaper and a fresh coat of paint on the trim around the windows and doors. There were filmy white curtains at the windows and gleaming hardwood on the floor. And, best of all, she'd brought up all her books from the basement and put them back on the shelves.

She closed the door and bounded down the stairs two at a time, yelling, "Bye, Mom. Bye, Dad," as she went.

She wheeled her bike out to the sidewalk. Her parents had worked hard on the outside of the house as well this summer. The front stairs had finally been replaced, the grass had been cut and the hedge trimmed. A big flower basket hung from the front porch. It looked like a house that somebody cared about. Not so much like a house from a scary movie anymore.

Jess adjusted her helmet and set off. The wind blew fresh against her face and a glorious feeling surged up inside her, a sense of elation and lightness. She looked up. High above, in the blue cloudless sky, she could see an eagle soar. Soaring! She felt like she was soaring too.

She had almost passed the house with the SOLD sign when she saw the van in the driveway. Someone was moving in. Jess jammed on the brakes. The front door of the house was open and there was a pile of cardboard boxes on the porch.

Then a girl appeared in the doorway. She jumped down the stairs and walked toward the van. She was about Jess' age, light brown hair in a ponytail. Shorts and a T-shirt. The girl pulled a box out of the van, heaved it into a more comfortable position and shuffled back toward the house. On the side of the box, in bold black letters, were the words MY BOOKS.

From inside the house, Jess heard a woman's voice call out.

"Sarah. Are you almost done?"

"Just about, Mom. Three or four more boxes and then I'm finished," the girl called back.

Jess watched from the sidewalk as the girl lurched up the stairs with the heavy box and disappeared into the house.

Jess leaned her bike against the fence and glanced down at the locket. Courage. Her legs felt like rubber and her heart was pounding. But she'd made up her mind. She opened the latch on the gate, walked straight up to the house and rang the doorbell.

AFTERWORD

Point Ellice House is a real house that was built in 1861. It sits on the banks of the Gorge Waterway in Victoria, British Columbia. The O'Reilly family lived at Point Ellice House for over a hundred years, from 1867 to 1975. The family kept everything during that time—everything from recipes, receipts and seed catalogues to clothing, furniture and artwork. Walking through the house today is like walking through a time capsule from the turn of the century. The house now operates as a museum during the summer months, Halloween (when they run a very spooky ghost tour) and at Christmas time.

The Point Ellice Bridge disaster occurred on May 26, 1896. An overloaded streetcar was on its way to the Victoria Day celebrations. The timbers in the bridge had rotted and could not support the weight of the streetcar. Fifty-five people died, making it the worst streetcar accident in North America.

There have been many ghost stories and ghost sightings at Point Ellice House and the bridge over the years. One of the oldest stories is about a strange, red light that appears near the bridge. Sightings of the red light are still reported to this day. *The Olden Days Locket* offers one possible explanation for this mysterious light.

Although Rose and Jess (as well as the Abbotts, Mrs. Cameron, and Mrs. Scott) are fictitious characters, the site and the historical background are not. The O'Reillys, Ellen, Sing, Moon and Mr. Norman were real people who lived or worked at Point Ellice House during that time. Very little is known about the servants other than their names and what they were paid. Their characters are entirely a product of my imagination.

This story is based on extensive research at Point Ellice House, the British Columbia Archives, the City of Victoria Archives, the Greater Victoria Public Library and the Heritage Branch Library. I am grateful for all the assistance I had from the Point Ellice House staff in researching this book. I have tried to make this story as authentic as possible, even to the weather each day (based on the O'Reilly diary entries). If you visit Point Ellice House today, it is possible to believe, with a little stretch of the imagination, that Rose and Jess' story may actually have happened.

FRANCES LITMAN

PENNY CHAMBERLAIN loves old houses, especially ones with ghosts. She lives in a ninety-year-old house on the outskirts of Victoria, B.C., and she is a member of the Friends of Point Ellice House. The Friends are currently working on restoring the dining room of Point Ellice House to its former grandeur at the turn of the century.

Penny was born in Nanaimo, B.C., and now works as a physiotherapist in Victoria. She is married to arts journalist Adrian Chamberlain, with whom she has a daughter, Katie. *The Olden Days Locket* is Penny's first novel.